No one c̲r̲  c̲e̲. I don't think Miss Em̲ t's hard to cry for someor̲ ut the old black people se̲c̲ ...y passed by her casket after the last prayer. And when Reverend Elton read the quote from Saint Theresa (Miss Emily's favorite saint), "Let nothing disturb you; let nothing frighten you. Everything passes except God. God alone is sufficient," all the black people there shouted a loud, "Amen!"

But the most intriguing thing of all was that gray-haired stranger who kept staring at the small headstone next to Miss Emily's grave that read, "Baby Boy, 1942," and who then stayed after everyone else had left. As we were leaving, I noticed from our car that the old man was crying. He picked a single yellow rose from the arrangement on top of Miss Emily's bronze casket and then gently placed it on the small grave, in front of the headstone. When Sally and I drove away, I looked back before we left the cemetery. The gentleman was limping away in the rain with his cane.

Before she died, Miss Emily had already disposed of most of her possessions, but there were two beautiful paintings and an antique rose vase still in her hospital room that she had left to Mrs. Brandon. She had given away all her clothes to a couple of nurses who promised they would take them to the Salvation Army for her, but I doubted that would happen. I remember commenting to Miss Emily years ago, when I was still a young lawyer, that a friend had once promised to retain our firm and then sought legal services elsewhere. Emily said, "Don't put too much stock in other people, David; they'll just disappoint you."

More about *THE RISING PLACE*

THE RISING PLACE was made into a film by Flatland Pictures and won sixteen film festival awards before opening in both New York and L.A. It is currently available on DVD.

The Rising Place

by

David McCall Armstrong

The Rising Place

Cover Art by *Debbie Taylor*

The Wild Rose Press, Inc.
PO Box 708
Adams Basin, NY 14410-0708
Visit us at www.thewildrosepress.com

Publishing History
First Mainstream Historical Edition, 2020
Print ISBN 978-1-5092-3065-5
Digital ISBN 978-1-5092-3066-2

Published in the United States of America

Dedication

To William and Canon—
the two greatest gifts God ever gave me

Introduction

When Emily Hodge died, I assumed I would be one of the few people at her funeral. She had lived such a solitary life. She didn't really seem like a loner, but that was before I learned about the murders and Miss Emily's past.

She had no family that I was ever aware of. Once, though, when I went to see her in the retirement center before she moved to the hospital, she said something about a "Mr. Wilder" who had visited her years earlier in Hamilton, when she used to live in her little yellow house. But I wasn't sure who this Wilder fellow was or where he was from, and I doubted he was still alive. That was a long time ago, like Miss Emily had said.

And that yellow frame house of hers on Monmouth Avenue has gone through several tenants since Miss Emily moved out and went to the Methodist Retirement Center. Most of the asbestos shingles on the front bottom of the house were covered now with kudzu vine and badly cracked, and Miss Emily would have hated they were so noticeable, so I never told her. I realized several years ago that there were some things it was best Miss Emily never know about.

I miss her yellow house, though. It has been vacant now for three years since the Bacons' grandson moved out and went back to college. The house had been just the right size for him—two bedrooms and one bath, with a large living/dining room combination off the kitchen, and the attic fan in the hall still worked after all these years. It was one of those small (Miss Emily called it "modest"), bungalow-style homes that Mr. Sinopoli came here and built in the late 1940s, right after World War II. Miss Emily once said that people didn't need much room back then. Young couples just married, or wives recently widowed from the War, didn't need more than two bedrooms, and when they had children, they just crowded them into the other bedroom.

I never understood why Miss Emily didn't marry and have her own children. She certainly was attractive enough in her younger days. She showed me an old picture of herself one Sunday afternoon at the General Hospital when I went by her room to visit for a few minutes after church. She was a "striking woman," as she herself commented. I certainly agreed. But it was more than just a striking young woman I saw in that faded, seventy-year-old photograph. She was beautiful. Standing on the running board of an old Ford, in a long, pink dress with a cream-colored flapper hat on her head, she reminded me of someone from that old Bonnie and Clyde movie. It was hard to believe the pretty young woman in the photo was her. I probably stared at it too long, and it seemed to make her uneasy that I thought she was so beautiful.

"You were a lovely girl," I awkwardly told her. When I handed the picture back to Miss Emily, she replaced it in a brown leather sewing box and slid it into the bottom drawer of the nightstand next to her bed. After she closed the drawer, I somehow knew Miss Emily would never show anyone that photograph of herself again.

Driving back home that Sunday afternoon, I couldn't get the picture of a young Miss Emily out of my mind. "God, she was a gorgeous woman," I said to myself. Maybe it's because I've always been attracted to brunettes, but I would have assumed any man would fall for the beautiful girl I saw in that picture. She had long, curly brown hair then that flowed out under her hat and onto her shoulders. And her dark brown eyes radiated with innocence. She was tall and thin, and the more I thought about that photograph of a pretty young brunette standing next to a Ford Edsel parked on a white sand beach somewhere, the less sense it made to me that Miss Emily Hodge would die alone.

When I moved down to Hamilton from New York—my wife, Sally, is originally from Mississippi— to begin my law practice with one of the oldest firms in the state, most of the cases assigned to me by Mr. Brandon, the senior partner in our firm, were the kind of legal cases only a new lawyer would handle. As I recall, they ranged from young black males accused of stealing from the stores they cleaned at night on Main Street to Emily Hodge's will. I remember the first time I ever saw her. Mr. Brandon drove me out to her house at 110 Monmouth Avenue while he told me a few things about her.

He said that Emily was an old friend of his wife, that she needed a will, and—almost apologetically— that he would appreciate my looking after her affairs since she had no one else. I don't recall anyone in Hamilton ever saying much more, if anything, about Emily Hodge. I just assumed she was a recluse. That's not unusual in a state like Mississippi. But the strange thing was, in a small town like Hamilton that prided itself on knowing everything about everybody, that a person like Miss Emily could have lived so unnoticed, so unknown—so, as Mr. Brandon put it, "forgotten."

Miss Emily was certainly not destitute. Quite the contrary. I soon discovered, after my first meeting with her, that she was, as people in the South say, "well-to-do." She owned a few stocks and bonds in addition to a respectable checking account which, for some reason, she never would convert into a savings account. I told Mr. Brandon that every time I advised her to put most of her money into an interest-bearing savings account, she merely replied, "Money is for spending—not for hoarding." So I finally quit bringing the subject up and concluded that Emily Hodge was the only person I ever knew who survived the Great Depression but didn't have a savings account. But back then I was an idealistic young attorney who hadn't realized yet that some people just don't fit the molds that society makes for them. And Miss Emily was one of those unique few who "heard all the instruments and saw all the colors."

I think I understood something else. Miss Emily was what people in the South still refer to as "old money." That doesn't necessarily mean you have a *lot* of money—in fact, often just the opposite. But these Southerners usually equate a person's social status, or the lack thereof, with how long money has been in one's family.

Strange, though.

I used to wonder where Miss Emily got her money. Other than her working part time at the Confederate History Museum in Woodridge several years ago, I never knew or heard of Miss Emily's ever being employed. But you must understand that "old money" means that you "came into" money. So I assumed Miss Emily must have inherited a substantial amount from her parents, after they died.

I do know she was an only child, and I inquired once of Curtis Beltzhoover, the president of First Hamilton Bank, as to the source of her inheritance. Curtis told me Emily Hodge's father had been a successful merchant and local politician whose wife left all their money to Emily. Maybe $100,000.00 isn't a lot of money when you live to be almost seventy-nine, but Emily had me direct in her will that all her estate, except for a few special bequests, would go to the First United Methodist Church of Hamilton. That was all she ever said about the matter, and I never questioned Miss Emily's directive.

On the day of the funeral, it started raining about eight o'clock that morning. It was to be only a short, graveside service—just like she wanted—with no open casket, and she specifically requested that no flowers be sent. It was the only request of hers I didn't honor. I couldn't bear the thought of that precious lady, who had lived and died all alone, being buried without flowers. It just wasn't right, so I ordered the finest arrangement of yellow roses I could find. I thought the color was appropriate, considering how much she loved her yellow house on Monmouth Avenue, and she always liked roses. As I've matured, I've learned that sometimes people want things but just don't know how to ask for them. I do believe Miss Emily would have liked those yellow roses.

I excused the small attendance at her service as due to the rain, but I didn't really expect many people from

Hamilton to attend. After Mr. Brandon's death a few years ago, the older members of our law firm had either retired or passed away. So I represented our firm at the funeral since no one else had any idea who Emily Hodge was. Curtis Beltzhoover had retired from the bank and moved to Biloxi to live with his son, Robert, and his family, so he was too old to make the four-hour drive back to Hamilton to attend. Most of Miss Emily's acquaintances had either passed on or were too old to go to a funeral on a rainy November morning. And since she had no relatives, it was only me, Reverend Elton from the Methodist Church, a few "regular funeral-goers," seven or eight old black men and women, Sally (who begged me not to make her go), and a handsome, gray-haired gentleman who was supporting himself with a walking cane. I had never seen him before.

It was a simple, Methodist prayer service that lasted only twenty minutes. Miss Emily had quit being a Roman Catholic years ago and had been "a Methodist since Eisenhower," as she liked to say. While she was still in good health and attending church, Miss Emily never would accept our invitation to sit with Sally and me and our two sons at the eleven o'clock service. She preferred, instead, to sit by herself in the third left row from the front. For some reason, she didn't enjoy the company of other women her own age and always worshiped alone. I wondered about this several times, but that simply was Miss Emily's way.

No one ever talked to Miss Emily, as I recall; she was merely regarded as best left alone. Strange, though, when I noticed her walking out of church one day, those sensitive brown eyes of hers didn't seem to belong to a spinster who preferred solitude. I thought then, and I certainly know now, that they were the tender eyes of a wounded soul. I had hoped someone else in our congregation might meet her eyes that day and offer a warm smile, as if to say, "I understand, dear lady. Yes, please come join us today for Sunday lunch." But no one ever smiled at Emily Hodge, much less ever invited her into their home.

No one cried during her funeral service. I don't think Miss Emily would have wanted that. It's hard to cry for someone you don't really know. But the old black people seemed to know her as they passed by her casket after the last prayer. And when Reverend Elton read the quote from Saint Theresa (Miss Emily's favorite saint), "Let nothing disturb you; let nothing frighten you. Everything passes except God. God alone is sufficient," all the black people there shouted a loud, "Amen!"

But the most intriguing thing of all was that gray-haired stranger who kept staring at the small headstone next to Miss Emily's grave that read, "Baby Boy, 1942," and who then stayed after everyone else had left. As we were leaving, I noticed from our car that the old man was crying. He picked a single yellow rose from the arrangement on top of Miss Emily's bronze casket and then gently placed it on the small grave, in front of the headstone. When Sally and I drove away, I looked back before we left the cemetery. The gentleman was limping away in the rain with his cane.

Before she died, Miss Emily had already disposed of most of her possessions, but there were two beautiful paintings and an antique rose vase still in her hospital room that she had left to Mrs. Brandon. She had given away all her clothes to a couple of nurses who promised they would take them to the Salvation Army for her, but I doubted that would happen. I remember commenting to Miss Emily years ago, when I was still a young lawyer, that a friend had once promised to retain our firm and then sought legal services elsewhere. Emily said, "Don't put too much stock in other people, David; they'll just disappoint you."

After a quick sandwich at my desk and after returning a few telephone calls, I drove to the hospital to retrieve Miss Emily's possessions. I was thinking about old Mrs. Brandon as I rode the elevator up to the third floor to Miss Emily's room—324—for the last time. I wondered, as I removed from the wall the small oil painting of rolling green hills covered with bluebonnet flowers, if Genevieve Brandon would appreciate the two fine paintings and the expensive vase that Miss Emily had bequeathed to her. I hadn't seen Mrs. Brandon in two years, not since her husband died, and I didn't remember Miss Emily ever talking much about her, but I recalled I had been told they used to be friends. But why didn't Mrs. Brandon at least send her regrets? It was strange to me that Miss Emily would leave those three valuable possessions to someone who neither attended her funeral nor sent her regrets. But I read once that Southerners like to keep things in the family. Maybe, since Miss Emily didn't have any family, she wanted her special possessions to pass to another old Hamilton family?

As I was about to turn out the light and leave her empty room, I remembered the brown sewing box of letters in the bottom drawer of the nightstand next to her bed. I also remembered that wonderful old photograph of her leaning against a car on the beach, which she had shown me several years ago. I didn't know why at the time, but I wanted that picture. I would keep it as a reminder of this dear lady I had come to love.

I didn't open the letter box until after I returned to my office and asked Dorothy Calhoun, Mr. Brandon's secretary, who still worked for our law firm, to carefully package the two paintings and the vase and take them to Mrs. Brandon's house.

In addition to the photograph of Miss Emily, there were several newspaper clippings about World War II and some other stories from the *Hamilton Times Herald* in the box. What intrigued me most, though, was the bundle of letters that were neatly addressed to "Harry Devening." They had been wrapped in brown twine, folded, stuffed, and stamped, and all of them had been resealed. It took me the rest of Friday afternoon and all weekend to read Miss Emily's letters. I don't know if she would have wanted me to read them since she was such a private person, but I do think I finally understand her now and why she died alone—but definitely not forgotten. I know I shall never forget her. How could I?

Book I

April 20, 1941
6:00 a.m.

My Dear Harry:

The bells of St. Ann's Cathedral are ringing as I write to you this morning. I know I have sinned—we both have sinned—so I will pray extra hard to Saint Theresa for us today.

I don't know where this letter of mine will find you, or if it will find you, for I don't know that I will ever mail it. All I know is that I love you and must see you again. I simply don't care what anyone thinks. I care what you think and what I think, and I care about what we had together and might yet have one day, God willing.

Is it wrong to feel as I do—to want you and desire you as I do? To desperately need you? To hold you in my arms again? If so, then I am wrong and bound for Hell! Mother certainly believes so, and I have no doubt that all her friends concur and comfort her in this regard. But if I am bound for Hell, then I can only hope—pray!—that you, my dear, will join me there. For most assuredly, I would prefer to spend eternity in Hell than to live forever without your love.

I apologize for this short letter, but I must go now to early Mass and pray for us both. My parents are waiting outside in the car for me. I will write to you again, my dear Harry. I must.

My love,
Emily

May 23, 1941

My Dear Harry:

It is strange what I observed today. You recall how affectionate Mary Beth Dearing and I have always been? And do you remember what she told me when we returned from Biloxi—that she would support me in whatever decision I made about our relationship? I saw her today at Jaber's Grocery, and she was so cool to me. Certainly not harsh or cruel, for Mary Beth is a perfect lady. But I sensed that she was embarrassed to be seen with me. What have I done to deserve this? Why would such a warm and close friend now shun me? I asked her, "Will you have lunch with me today?"

"No, I must visit my aunt this afternoon. Danny and I promised her that we would call today since she has been ill. I'm sorry, Emily."

That was all we said to one another. Short and formal. I know what she was thinking, though, and I hate it. God knows how I hate the prejudice in this town! First toward you, my love, and now toward me. As if I am no longer one of them—not good enough for their company. It is so wrong.

My love,
Emily

June 12, 1941

My Dear Harry:

It is apparent now that everyone knows about us. Since you left for Camp Shelby, these past seven weeks have been horrible. I miss you unbearably, uncontrollably—almost unforgivably. Yet, I know you had to leave.

Perhaps we were wrong to have fallen in love. Perhaps I was wrong to have seduced you. Yes, I admit it! This love, this whole affair, was my fault. I have confessed my sin to God many times, but I swear before God that I cannot forget you. I love you too much. Despite it all—the stares, the insidious remarks they think I cannot hear but do; despite the coldness and aloofness of my former friends, even despite that I have embarrassed my dear father and mother so—

I do love you,
Emily

June 18, 1941

My Dear Harry:

How long has it been now? Two months since you left, since I last beheld your precious face? Though I have heard nothing from you, I do understand.

I know this terrible fighting overseas is not to your liking—you who are so gentle and kind. I cannot bear the thought of your possibly being engaged in such an awful conflict, and I pray that President Roosevelt will not get this nation involved. I cannot and will not allow myself to think that any harm might befall you.

I say a Rosary and pray every evening to Saint Theresa that she will keep you safe, should we ever go to the defense of Great Britain. Despite my sin, I do believe she hears me.

How I remember your last night here—that drive with you through Dillon Park. I have replayed the scene in my mind a hundred times. Do you remember where we parked Mother's Edsel under that pine tree, next to the pavilion? Well, I heard today that the city is going to clear those woods for a public golf course. I cannot believe they would cut down all those beautiful trees! I told Father that, as an alderman, he must prevent such a travesty. He said I was too headstrong—can you believe that? I do intend to protest this matter, though, as I cannot bear the idea of our lovely park being destroyed so a few old men can play golf.

How utterly preposterous!

I cannot go on like this. I must come out and tell you. I cannot lie and say I merely wrote to tell you about this golf course matter. I am pregnant.

It must have happened that night before you left, when we returned to your apartment. I don't know what to do. There is no one but you and Saint Theresa with whom I can share this news. I pray that I am wrong, and may God strike me dead for not being thankful for carrying a child conceived from our love.

But how will I ever stand this disgrace alone? What sort of life would this child have here? He or she would never be accepted in this town. God knows that. I am already no longer accepted, merely for having loved you. But a child born out of wedlock and part Negro? It would be intolerable!

Could I have prevented this from happening? Could I have prevented myself from falling in love with you? These are the questions I ask God to answer. Yet what does it matter now? I must get some sleep. Maybe God will take me in my slumber, and this life—our life—inside me will never know the shame and guilt that I now feel. How unfair this would be to our child. Please let me hear from you. I miss you terribly.

Emily

July 13, 1941

My Dear Harry:

I try to stay as busy as I can. During the day, I am involved in a church project which occupies my time. We lost the "Battle of the Woods," as those of us opposed to the golf course development called it. I was able to organize a small group of people that asked Mayor Burns and the Board of Aldermen to not allow our trees to be aborted, but to no avail. Their awful project will be done, despite all our erstwhile efforts.

I never get to the issue at hand, do I? I am now a public spectacle. I am three months pregnant. I am seeing old Doctor Ernst, but I can tell he would prefer I go to someone else for checkups. (His wife is such a snob!) I also embarrass his nurse, Mrs. Barnes. I'm at the point now where I can usually sense things like this.

This pregnancy has nearly killed my father. You probably remember my saying he wanted to run for mayor against Elmo Burns this fall. What a joke that now would be! I cannot stand how this has hurt him and Mother, and I do hate myself for my present situation. But I trust God and know He will resolve this matter according to His will. He always does.

Still, this is such a heavy cross to carry. My parents hardly entertain now. Our house seemed so sad this Fourth of July. They don't even go to the Country Club anymore, and Father has abandoned his Wednesday night poker group with his old Catholic buddies. It is all my fault.

I live with my guilt and shame every day. But I mentioned earlier that I try to stay busy. There are so many causes that need pursuing in a town like this—so much to do that I have become "proud" of myself, despite my predicament. If I am to be shunned by society, then certainly I can help others less fortunate than me. And if I am to be regarded as an outcast (a "loathsome person," as someone referred to me in an anonymous letter) who loved a man with a Negro grandmother, then I resolve to do as much good with my life as I possibly can.

My Love,
Emily

August 17, 1941

Dear Harry:

My new friend Wilma and I drove up to Vicksburg today because I had to get out of town. I am showing now, but I make no pretense about it anymore. Ironically, I am pretty much "old news," anyway.

"Not really," Wilma said, but it does help me to believe that I am. People do not stare at me anymore; they simply look away. Genevieve Brandon crossed to the other side of Main Street yesterday when she saw me coming. That probably hurt me as much as anything ever has. But I forgive her. Associating with me would kill her husband's chances of making partner in his new law firm. That is important; our friendship is not. I do miss her, though, and I somehow believe she misses me. Just a woman's intuition, I guess.

Wilma told me her mother said that Hitler person is doing horrible things to the Jewish people in Europe. Her mother is quite literate and aware of all the news and local gossip. I do not know her father and probably will never meet him. I am not sure if Wilma even knows him since she never speaks of him. I have yet to broach the subject of her father with her for fear I might lose her friendship—now, it seems, my only one.

I don't believe you ever met Wilma. I guess it's not likely you would have associated with her during your brief few months in Hamilton.

I have told Wilma much about you, though, my dear.

I told her you were twenty-three years old and that you moved here from Indiana to work for the Power Company. (Why you chose to move to a place like Hamilton, though, I will never understand.) And I told her I met you at your company's fish fry out at the Steam Plant with my father. I told her how forward you first seemed to me, but Wilma assured me all Yankee men were that way. Notwithstanding, I told Wilma you were so handsome—tall, with black hair and the darkest eyes I've ever seen. You're truly the finest man I have ever met—not like these boyish fools I know here in Hamilton.

I confessed to you then that I had dated before but had never known another man. I swear to you now that I will *never* know another man. I cannot expect the same fidelity from you, I know. But please, *please* come back to me! The thought of living the rest of my life without you is just too much. I will gladly bear your child, but I cannot bear living life without you.

I Love You!

Emily

September 9, 1941

My Dear Harry:

Wilma came to the back door this morning, and we had coffee outside on the patio. She fears being seen walking up our steps in the front of the house, so she came down Newman Street and cut through the Reeds' back yard into ours. How silly I told her she is, but Wilma said, "Too many white folks think you're a 'n——lover,' Emily," and she doesn't want me to be hurt anymore. I told Wilma not to ever use that disgusting term again, and I meant it!

With all the horrible atrocities going on across the ocean, you would think these provincial people here would have something better to do than gossip about me!

I am five months pregnant now, but I don't want to burden you about this matter because it really is my responsibility. I have reconciled my dilemma with God, though I feel sure He is still angry with me, but how can I ever forgive myself for not being more careful?

You who are wonderful and mean everything in the world to me shouldn't have to deal with this burden of my flesh too. You may soon be engaged in a great cause, I truly believe. I understand now why you do not write back. But please, my dear, do not be mad at me.

Wilma and I discussed this morning what should name our little child. Certainly, if the child is born a boy, we should call him "Harry"—after you. (There really is no other name in the world I would even consider!) If our child is born a little girl, I particularly like the name "Theresa," since that is the name of my favorite saint. Please write and tell me what you think.

My Love,
Emily

September 12, 1941

My Dear Harry:

In my letter of August 17th, I spoke of my fondness for Wilma as if you knew her. How silly of me to forget you haven't met her yet.

She is the most intelligent Negro I have ever known and the best friend I have ever had. She has pale-green eyes and very light features, and she always pulls her silky black hair back with a green bow. She is only a frail and tiny girl of eighteen, but Wilma Watson has such a valiant spirit. I know you would love her too, certainly not because she is colored, but because of her goodness and strength.

How hypocritical we people here are; we are so quick to judge others by the color of their skin and their heritage. What a great shame that someone like you would be ostracized here, simply because you are one-quarter Negro. Wilma tells me that to the white people of Hamilton, you may as well be "full-n——," but I really wish Wilma would stop using that awful word. I don't mean to offend you with all this, and you certainly have enough to worry about, but I am greatly agitated by all this bigotry in our town.

Then when I read of all the horrors being done by that evil man Adolph Hitler, I long to run away to some world where hatred does not exist. Will you go with me, my love? I know I am naïve, but is it wrong to be an idealist? Why can't people just leave other folks alone?

I dread the thought of bringing a child into a world that is so sick with hatred and bigotry. What kind of life would this child have here? To be born one-eighth Negro in Hamilton, Mississippi—though that is really nothing—would be a crime against their society. I overheard Mrs. Geisenberger telling Mother the other day how hard it was for her husband to have lived here, being Jewish, and that what is happening now to all his relatives in Berlin and other places in Germany would have been too much for him to bear. She said that she's glad Mr. Geisenberger is not still alive to see it.

I must fight all this. I must do something to combat all the inhumanity that I see. My life is not worth much, for I have sinned greatly. But with all my might and soul, I must rise up for what is right. This I will do for the sake of our child and for the love that I feel for you.

Emily

September 18, 1941

My Dear Harry:

It's 5:00 in the morning, and I have been awake for two hours. I am very ill. I haven't told you in any previous letter of the complications I have had during this time, since I did not want to bother you. The morning sickness will eventually pass, and I have no doubt this present discomfort will only make me stronger. So do not worry over me, my dear.

Everything is so quiet here. I really love this old house—even with all its squeaks and despite that it is so humid in here this time of year.

When you're awake this early in the morning—even though you seem all alone in the world—it really is quite pleasant. How I wish you were here beside me, though. That would be like heaven.

I dream of you every night. I dreamed last night we were flying in the Phoenix again. How I so much enjoyed that day with you.

I was so impressed when you told me you were a pilot! I don't know why I doubted you at first, but I had always been afraid of flying, and it's hard for me to conceive of my fear being someone else's passion. But you were so patient with me that first time. And after I strapped into my seat behind you and saw how in control you were—I believe that is when I first fell in love with you. I'm not sure if I even thanked you for helping me to not be afraid. That is why I do so now, my love.

And though I was terrified while we were taking off, when we left the ground and began to fly—TO FLY!—I became a part of you and what you loved: that marvelous airplane you called "the Phoenix." Oh, to be transported through the clouds by the man you love! I had no fears—no anxiety—only total trust in you. And it seemed as though I lost all consciousness, except now, for the memory of that glorious moment—flying, as it seemed, forever.

I hear a distant train outside. I've always loved the sound of a train whistle passing by. Such a solace; it reminds me of you. And how I'd love to be on that train now, on my way to see you.

Have you been accepted yet into the Army Air Corps? I know this was your dream, and they would be so fortunate to have such a wonderful pilot as you.

I asked Father last night if he thought we should go to the defense of Great Britain, since that country is our closest ally.

"Don't be too quick to want to fight," he told me. "That's their war, not ours."

"Surely we can't just sit around and watch and do nothing?" I replied.

"I don't trust Roosevelt," Father then told Mother and me. Mother didn't say anything; she just kept doing her needlepoint.

"I think President Roosevelt is a good man," I told them both, "and I *do* trust him."

"He's too liberal for me, and I wish he'd quit meeting with those Japanese. They're not to be trusted. History has already proven that." That was all we said on the matter. I turned on the radio and listened to Jack Benny, and Father went outside to smoke his cigar.

I am concerned about this "War in Europe." (That's what Father and the other men who get together to discuss it at McGuire's Grill every morning call it.) I'm glad Father is being more sociable now. He's going out with his friends again, and I think the subject of "Emily" doesn't come up quite so often anymore. My situation seems to have taken a back seat to this present conflict. I am glad for that, but I'm truly worried about what probably awaits this country.

It is awful to fear the future. But being concerned for you and the fate of others, I can quit being so selfish and concerned about myself.

Wilma said to tell you hello. The picture that I enclose is of her. I told her the green bow in her hair is pretty and rounds out her skinny face. Wilma thinks it makes her look like a little girl. How silly of her.

I hear Father walking down the hall outside my room. It is time for me to get up and get going. I have so much to do today.

All my love,

Emily

P.S. I forgot to mention that my father isn't the only one I know who thinks President Roosevelt is too liberal.

Will Bacon, for what his opinion is worth, feels the same way. Will swears that Roosevelt is somehow going to get us involved in this conflict and then draft him to go fight. I pray that Will is wrong on both counts.

September 25, 1941

Dear Harry:

I heard today the National Guard is taking over our airport. Mayor Burns announced over the local broadcast station that no more private flights will be allowed out there because the Guard must train, in case of war with the Germans.

And there was an article in the *Hamilton Times Herald* that Camp Shelby in Hattiesburg may send Army Air Corps troops up here to help the Guard train! How my heart leapt for joy when I read this, in hopes that you might be with them! Could this possibly be true?

I await your reply, but waiting to hear a word from you—any word!—is the hardest thing I've ever had to do. When will you write? Please let me know if you will be coming back soon. I love you so much.

Emily

September 29, 1941

Dear Harry:

Yesterday in Mass, I prayed that you will be coming back here with the unit from Camp Shelby. It is exciting to think I might soon be in your arms again, embraced by your love. I dream to look into your eyes and relive what we had together while you were here, those glorious few months. My fondest memory is when you flew me over the river in the Phoenix, and we landed in that abandoned field near Somerset. Do you recall what a gorgeous day it was? The sun was so bright—it felt like we were soaring straight up into its rays! And now I understand why you love that airplane so much and why you must fly.

I cannot describe my pleasure in watching you at those controls. How smoothly you soared up through the clouds. And how I would have flown with you anywhere in that airplane—perfectly content to fly with you forever, as I've written you before.

When we landed—I never told you this—I was disappointed that we had touched down. I know this sounds silly, but to be carried through the clouds by the man you love is total ecstasy, and I shall cherish that day forever!

Do you remember what we discussed after we landed and made love on my blanket? You seemed to sense you wouldn't be in Hamilton for much longer.

You told me how much you wanted to go back home, where you belonged, how you were resented for being a Yankee and that your boss at the Steam Plant had found out you were part Negro.

Oh, I almost forgot to tell you—Will Bacon asked about you the other day. I saw him outside the old Grand Theatre, as Wilma and I were leaving.

"How's your friend, Harry? He should be getting a leave soon."

"I hope so, Will, and he's fine."

Will didn't say anything about the baby, but I'm sure he knows you are the father. I suspect it is common knowledge in Hamilton. It's funny, though, that I'm not the topic of much gossip anymore. After being relegated to the status of a Jezebel these past few months, it really doesn't bother me now. But I'm sure Will Bacon knows. I know he'll say something about it, sooner or later.

I do believe Will was fond of you, and I think he rather likes me. He treats me like a person instead of white trash—like most of my other "acquaintances" do. Wilma, Lord love her, is somewhat skeptical of Will. Honestly, she thinks he's just a "little sissy."

"Why else wouldn't Will Bacon have already enlisted?" she asked me the other day.

"You know Will has to take care of his momma," I reminded her.

"That's a mighty easy excuse. You'd think he'd be more concerned about fighting for his country than taking care of that lazy momma of his."

"That's just him, Wilma—you know that."

I don't know if I told you in one of my previous letters, but Wilma is quite opinionated. I have warned her about this, for Wilma is getting involved in some political issues at her church that I really wish she would stay away from. But I do love her, and she is so good to me.

But I ramble so much in these letters, don't I? I read in *Reader's Digest* last week that pregnant women often do this. So please forgive me for not sticking to my main purpose in writing.

You also told me that day in the landing field that your greatest dream was to fly. I have prayed for your dream to come true. Though I have not heard, I can only assume you have been accepted into the Army Air Corps, for they would be foolish to turn down such a wonderful pilot as you. Father told me Camp Shelby is a training ground now for new Army pilots, so my special prayer to Saint Theresa, and I pray to her every night, is that your dream has become a reality and that you are flying one of those new Army airplanes.

I must be selfish and admit that *my* dream—my soul's greatest longing—is for your unit to be sent up here to train our National Guard boys how to fly.

Will you come back here if you are asked? You told me in the landing field, after we finished our lunch and drank the wine you brought, that you had to get out of Hamilton. How I wanted to run away with you. I wouldn't have hesitated to have gotten back in the Phoenix and flown away with you to anywhere.

I don't blame you for not wanting to return here, though. I am much different now than when you left. But my love for you is unchanged.

Emily

October 11, 1941

Dear Harry:

We received news yesterday of a terrible accident that happened at Fort Sill, Oklahoma. Mary Beth Dearing's younger brother, Danny, was killed in an artillery explosion along with two other soldiers. My parents and I went over to the Dearings' house last night; they are all devastated. Thankfully, lots of people were there.

Danny was such a fine young man, and he had high hopes of playing football at Ole Miss when his enlistment was up. Mary Beth told me she feared the worst when she saw the telegraph boy walking up her front steps yesterday morning. I am afraid many American families will soon come to dread receiving *any* type of telegraph.

The thought of losing a loved one, like Mary Beth has now lost her brother, is incomprehensible to me. I could tell Mary Beth and her mother had been crying all day, but Mr. Dearing seemed strangely unmoved— almost like he didn't believe his only son had just been killed. He has always been such a strong man, though. I don't know if you ever met Mr. Dearing, but Father told me later he had never seen Mr. Dearing express any kind of emotion, so it didn't surprise him that Mr. Dearing didn't cry over Danny's death. I don't think Father especially cares for Mr. Dearing, though, since he's a big Roosevelt supporter, but he promised he would say an extra prayer tonight for the repose of Danny's soul.

I must question why God would allow such a fine Catholic boy like Danny Dearing to die so young. It doesn't seem fair, and it almost makes me question my faith when the good are allowed to die. Why would God not take, instead, an evil man like Adolf Hitler? Surely, He won't allow this monster to continue murdering the poor Jewish people in Europe. It is hard to reconcile and continue to pray every day to a God who seems not to care about who lives and who dies.

I visited with Father Bruni, our new priest from Italy, after Mass last Sunday, and I asked him why God does not intervene to save His own people, the Jews.

Father Bruni replied, rather coldly I thought, "Don't forget that it was the Jews who persecuted and murdered our Lord and Savior."

"So…are you saying, Father, that God is getting revenge on the Jews?"

"I am saying," he told me, "that we must all account for our deeds."

"But these Jewish people didn't kill Jesus."

"Miss Hodge, you should never question God's judgment. We all have sinned."

What did he mean by that? I know I have sinned, and even an old priest can tell that I'm six months pregnant! But why would he try to make me feel guilty? I'm appalled that Father Bruni didn't have more sympathy for those poor Jews. And they're not to blame; they never have been. Priests aren't God!

This is no way to end a letter, but I keep thinking about poor Danny Dearing. Certainly, he never sinned enough to deserve being blown half in two! Perhaps Father Bruni feels Danny was being punished because of some sin his grandfather committed? This is all so distressing.

I had to get away today. Wilma and I drove over the new bridge into Louisiana this morning and went out to the landing field in Somerset. I often dream about that place; I love it so much. I am safe there. Always happy. In my dreams, you and I are always together, lying on my red blanket next to the Phoenix, embraced in each other's arms.

I wanted to picnic there today with Wilma, as we did last spring. The leaves are so beautiful this time of the year, and it was such a gorgeous day. But it wasn't the same without you.

We had to take Will Bacon along with us. We stopped at Jaber's Grocery to gas up and get a few soft drinks, and Will was in there talking Mr. Jaber's ear off. Will really is so arrogant. He was bragging about applying to West Point and trying to explain why he hadn't enlisted yet. Mr. Jaber may be old, but he isn't stupid.

Actually, I was afraid some of those old farmers in there were going to hurt Will due to all the lies he was telling, so I invited him to leave and join Wilma and me. He didn't ride with us, but he followed us to the landing field in his mother's car. You should have heard Wilma. She was fit to be tied and shook her tiny head the whole way over there for my inviting Will Bacon to join us. You know, I don't think Wilma likes him. He's sweet, though, and he's totally harmless.

I noticed a couple of those farmers staring at me while I was paying for our soft drinks. One of them, in a filthy pair of overalls, was looking me up and down like I was a horse he wanted to buy. And I know he made some remark like "n——lover" as I was walking out.

Wilma said her momma knows him from years back. I think she said his name is "Scruggs" and that he works Negroes down on his farm at Pine Bluff like they were still slaves. What a mean-looking, ugly old man he was. You could see the hatred in his bloodshot eyes. He was fat and sweaty, and his body odor was horrible. I'm sure he's the most despicable person I've ever encountered.

But Wilma is so funny. Despite how afraid of him I was, she made me laugh. I think that's why I love her so—she helps me to forget myself. When we were driving away with prissy Will Bacon following us, Wilma remarked, "I bet we just made that old redneck's day—a n——, a Jezebel, and a sissy—Lord, ain't we a threesome!"

Driving down that long dusty road toward the landing field, I couldn't help but believe that Wilma was probably right. But I really do hate that word.

I still love you,
Emily

P.S. I will tell you more tomorrow; it is late. Please write and let me know whether you will be coming with the Camp Shelby unit next month. I really must get everything ready for your arrival.

Love,
Emily

October 12, 1941
6:00 a.m.

Dear Harry:

I wrote you last night about driving over to the landing field with Wilma and Will Bacon. It took us longer than the usual twenty minutes to get there. The cars on that farm road that turns off the highway were bumper to bumper. We passed the Carroll twins on the way. Bob is such a gentleman, but I never could abide Greg Carroll. It's common knowledge he got Olivia Meng pregnant, but Wilma quickly reminded me that I am no one to be pointing fingers.

Most of the automobiles on that road were also headed to the landing field. It was such a lovely day, and I was thrilled to see all the airplanes that were parked on the field, getting ready to fly. There is so much excitement around Hamilton, and I have noticed a lot more people in town these past weeks who have come to enlist in the National Guard. They've already taken over Hargis Airport, so most of the local fliers are grounding over at Somerset.

It seems all the young men want to be pilots. Mrs. Sullivan, who lives down the street from us, has already taken in three new recruits from Woodridge who moved here to enlist and train. Will Bacon said the Ford Hotel downtown is full, and he heard Mayor Burns say at school assembly last Wednesday that the Guard is asking local families to put up new recruits while permanent barracks are being built at the airport. Hamilton has come alive with all this war talk and work, but I do pray it is only temporary. I think some people believe this is only a child's game. Sometimes I want to write an article in the *Times Herald* and remind them about poor Danny Dearing. But it's so easy to forget about reality and get swept away by all the furor and excitement.

It was such a grand sight at the landing field to watch those airplanes take off and land. I counted nine planes that day, and there must have been forty to fifty people out on the field picnicking with us. How I missed you, though. It just wasn't the same to see the Phoenix take off and fly without you at the controls. And how I longed to be in that airplane with you, flying through the clouds again. I know I am a dreamer, but how my soul yearns to be with you. Perhaps one blessed day, after this horrible conflict is over and you have returned, we can fly away with our child to some distant world and live forever. What true bliss that would be, my love.

It was strange when the Phoenix returned from a short flight and landed close to where we were—under that same live oak tree in the corner by the fence. I didn't know who her pilot was, and I certainly wouldn't have bothered to inquire, but Will Bacon said, "Emily, do you know who is flying the Phoenix today?"

"I don't care who's flying her, Will. All I know is that it isn't Harry in that airplane."

"That's Dr. O'Brien's son, Thomas. Harry sold that airplane to Dr. O'Brien right before he left. Remember?"

"Yes, I remember, Will. And I think Dr. O'Brien took advantage of Harry because he was leaving town."

Then Will Bacon added, "Because he *had* to leave town, don't you mean?"

I've never struck another human being in my life, but I almost slapped Will Bacon when he made that stupid remark. Wilma just laughed and said, "At least Harry's not still at home taking care of his momma, Will."

I don't think Will Bacon comprehended Wilma's admonition. For someone who brags about being so intelligent and applying to West Point, Will Bacon certainly is insensitive.

"Is Harry coming up with the Camp Shelby unit, Emily?" Will asked after taking a swallow of Coke and a long drag from his Lucky Strike cigarette.

"I don't know, Will."

"Of course he's coming back here, Will Bacon!" Wilma butted in and said, "And when Harry gets here, me and Emily and him are going for a ride in one of those big green Army planes that Momma showed me a picture of in the paper on Sunday."

"That's ridiculous, Wilma," Will said, "and don't be such a sassy little wench. Hell, I can't even believe I'm out here with you two, sitting on this blanket. Lord, half the people I know in Hamilton are over here!"

"What's wrong, Will Bacon?" Wilma asked him. "You 'fraid it might hurt your reputation, being seen with a couple of girls?"

I had to laugh out loud at that. Will Bacon took a quick, dramatic drag from his cigarette, then he said, "I would think you two 'low-lifes' would be honored to be with me today."

I had to respond. "With you? Good heavens, Will—if I hadn't rescued you from Jaber's Grocery Store, you'd probably be half-dead by now! I don't think Mr. Scruggs was impressed with all your stories."

"I don't think that old fool, with all due respect to his noble profession, has ever left the farm. And I'm quite sure he's never even heard of West Point. I'm not afraid of him—or his moronic son, Eddie, either."

"Will Bacon," I said, "Please be serious. Are you really trying to go to West Point? My father asked me the other night after dinner, and I told him that—"

"I can speak for myself, Emily, if you don't mind. And I will address our inquisitive alderman on this matter personally, the next time I see him. By the way, how come your daddy decided not to run for mayor?"

"Really now, Will," I said. "What do you think? That is, assuming you think at all."

"I think he would have probably gotten all the colored vote," Will quipped.

Wilma and Will both thought that was funny, and I had to laugh myself, despite the fact I think Will Bacon is such a little twerp.

The air show that day was wonderful, though all three of us agreed no pilot there was as good as you. I didn't like the way Thomas O'Brien flew the Phoenix. He didn't seem like he knew how to handle her. He almost tipped the left wing too low on his second landing. Will Bacon said Thomas is much too young to be flying anyway since he's only seventeen, like Will.

Everyone left about 4:00. How deserted that field seemed as the cars began driving away, one by one. Will Bacon made some excuse about not being able to help Wilma and me pack up—he claimed he had to hurry back into town to Lea's Drugstore before it closed at five o'clock to buy some medicine for his momma.

I never know whether to believe Will—he always exaggerates so much. Wilma said her momma told her that Mrs. Bacon hits the bottle heavy and early, so Will was probably going to buy some whiskey for her. But I didn't think anyplace in Hamilton would sell whiskey to a minor, did you?

Wilma said a pregnant woman like me shouldn't be so naïve. "Girl," she said, "you're about to bring a brand-new baby into this awful world, so it's time for you to wake up and open those pretty brown eyes of yours to what's going on. Besides," she said, "Momma says we might go to war with Germany, so youth don't matter no more." What a horrible thought that was for me to have to consider.

I know that Wilma's momma is probably right, and I guess if you're old enough to fight and die, then you're old enough to buy whiskey.

Love,
Emily

October 12, 1941
10:45 p.m.

My Dear Harry:
Mother and Father were in the front parlor waiting for me when I came downstairs about eight o'clock this morning. I could tell something was wrong.

Father stood up abruptly before I could even say "Good morning" and announced, "We must talk now, Emily—something has happened."

I got a sick feeling in my stomach when he said that—just like when I first realized I was pregnant. It's such a strange, helpless feeling when you think you're about to hear something bad. Your mind races backward, trying desperately to remember what you've said or done wrong.

"Were you and Will Bacon together yesterday?"

I thought before I answered because I wasn't sure what he was getting at.

"Yes. Why?"

"Sit down, Emily. Your mother and I need to talk to you."

"Has something happened to Will?" I asked them both.

"Will Bacon has been in an accident, Emily," Mother told me.

Father interrupted, "No, Rebecca, it wasn't an accident. Will was intentionally attacked." Then he looked straight at me and said, "Will Bacon was beaten up late yesterday afternoon, pretty badly. They had to take him to the General Hospital."

"My God, Father—why? Who would do such a mean thing to Will Bacon? He's only a kid."

"He's almost eighteen, Emily!" my mother said sharply. "Most of his classmates have already enlisted in the Army or the Navy, or are at least preparing to!"

"So that's a good reason to hurt someone, Mother?" I asked her indignantly. "Besides, he's trying to get into West Point. Or didn't those thugs who attacked him know that?"

Neither Mother nor Father said anything in reply. I could tell they didn't believe Will Bacon had actually applied to the Military Academy any more than I did. So I said to both of them, "Who were these ruffians that attacked Will? Have they been caught?"

"I don't believe, dear, that they will be caught," Father said.

"What? You mean the sheriff isn't out looking for them? Why not?"

"I spoke with Sheriff Creel before you came down, dear," Father said. "They were local boys—three of them. Creel knows who they are."

"Then why hasn't he arrested them? I seriously doubt they can claim they attacked Will Bacon in self-defense."

"Emily, dear," Mother said, "Will Bacon brought this on himself. They said he went into Jaber's Grocery to steal a bottle of liquor."

"I don't believe that, Mother. I'm sorry to dispute you, but I just can't accept that. Who did you hear that story from?"

"A quite reliable source, I assure you."

"So you *were* with Will yesterday," Father stated.

"Yes, I already told you. What difference does that make?"

"It makes a lot of difference!" Mother yelled at me. "How do you think it makes us feel, knowing that our pregnant daughter has been cavorting all day with a Negro and a little sissy who's also a *thief*? Haven't you already embarrassed us enough?"

That was all I could stand. I guess I had sensed for some time how embarrassed my mother was to have a daughter like me, but I had never heard her actually say it before.

Tonight, I prayed for Will Bacon and that God would one day forgive me for the grief I have caused my parents. I cried in my pillow until I finally fell asleep.

How I miss you and need you more than ever.

Emily

October 13, 1941

Dear Harry:

The *Hamilton Times Herald* reported today that a local youth had been apprehended while shoplifting from Jaber's Grocery. That was all it said. No story. No details. Nothing. There was no mention that Will Bacon had been severely beaten after he left the store, and the only other thing the article said was that Mr. Jaber would not press charges since the two-dollar bottle of Red Crow whiskey was returned to him by Eddie Scruggs. Eddie and two of his cousins "just happened" to be waiting outside the store when Will Bacon was trying to "escape."

I don't believe a word of it. And even though Wilma doesn't like Will, she doesn't believe it either.

I ate a quick bowl of cereal this morning and left the house early, barely even speaking to my parents. Then I borrowed Mother's car and drove out past the Hamilton Junior College to Wilma's house. I wanted to see if she had heard what happened to Will Bacon.

It was the first time I had ever visited Wilma's house. That's hard for me to believe, though, because Wilma and I have spent so much time together these past few months. As I've told you before, not only is Wilma my only friend now, she's my only confidant.

It's so different in the north part of town—out past the college in the Negro section. Almost as if the

Southern Line railroad tracks are the dividing place between colored and white. Do you remember how we joked that night about getting married in a railway car right over the middle of the tracks—just to please our families? I don't think my mother would have invited any of her Garden Club friends to such a ceremony, though. Don't you agree?

I fear I have greatly hurt her. Why, if she knew I had driven her car over to the Negro side of town, she would be appalled!

Isn't that so ridiculous? I mean, aside from the obvious bigotry of it all, everyone in town already knows I made love to a man of part-color. It's as though she doesn't even realize I'm pregnant! What a silly woman I sometimes think she is. God forgive me for feeling this way (and dear Saint Theresa knows I do love my mother), but how can I respect a woman who is more concerned with her reputation than my feelings? I am sorry I have sinned, and I'm sorry I embarrassed my parents and ruined my father's political future, but I truly don't care about those kinds of things anymore.

I am more concerned about the unfairness of it all. To me, those blue-haired old ladies who live in their antebellum homes on the south side of town should come see the poverty on the north side of the tracks. I am preaching now, I know, but it broke my heart to see all those Negro families out there with nothing at all. No electricity. No running water. Old, rundown wooden shacks leaning against each other on a narrow dirt road you can't even drive your car down. I intend to speak to Father about this. I realize he doesn't represent this part of Hamilton, but it's disgraceful that our city leaders won't even run a sewer line out there.

Oh, Harry, it was simply awful! I can't bear to realize these poor people actually live that way! What kind of society are we to allow this? We can't simply turn our backs and ignore such poverty and deprivation. I *will* not!

And when I finally got to Wilma's little house, it was all I could do to keep from crying. I was so ashamed that we have so much, and they have almost nothing.

Her house looked like it had grown up and squeezed itself between the two shanties next to it. It was so tiny. It reminded me of a small weed that had sprouted between two old bricks out in a yard. I simply can't imagine how Wilma, her four brothers and sisters, and her momma can all live in such a small, wretched abode. I do understand now why she never invited me to her house. Wilma has always been honest with me, but I don't think she was forthright in telling me to not come out here "because a white lady like you shouldn't be seen in this part of town," she claimed. I believe she was simply embarrassed over her living situation. The poor thing.

Did she actually think I would care less for her because she wasn't as blessed as I am? I love Wilma for who she is inside, not for what she has, and she is as good and decent as any white person I know. I must convince Wilma of this fact, for she is truly special.

Yet I could not help being embarrassed for her. The tin roof on their little shack was falling off, and there were several boards missing on the front porch. There was no grass in the tiny front yard, and the four chickens they kept fenced in weren't even fit to eat.

"We're trying to fatten them up for Thanksgiving."

Wilma laughed as she told me that later.

"Come on in, Miss Emily," Wilma's momma, Geneva, said as she stood at the front door. "What brings you out to this part of town, and why you here so early? I'll go wake Wilma."

"Who's that outside, Momma?" I heard Wilma call from the back part of the house.

"Come on in here, child," Geneva told me. "I'll boil some coffee for us and slice some fresh bread."

"Emily, is that you?" Wilma hollered.

"Yes, Wilma. I apologize for coming unannounced so early in the morning, but I had to see you. It's about Will Bacon. Have you heard what happened to him?"

Wilma walked into the tiny kitchen. She was still half asleep and was wearing a green flannel robe, but she didn't have any slippers on her small bare feet. That pinewood floor had to be cold. She sat on the table bench, yawned, and just stared at me for a few moments.

Geneva had overheard Mr. and Mrs. Greer, who Geneva cooks and cleans for, discussing Will Bacon late yesterday afternoon, and she'd told Wilma about it last night, I learned.

Wilma said, "Yep, Will Bacon was definitely lying to us when he said he was going to get his momma some medicine from Lea's Drugstore. I didn't believe a word, Emily, no, ma'am! I knew he wasn't telling us the truth, and I knew exactly where he was headed when he prissed outta there and spun off in that old Plymouth of his mother's like a n—— running from the Klan."

I heard Geneva laughing to herself in the kitchen while she boiled coffee on the wood stove. (That word must not bother Geneva, either.) Then Wilma added, "Yes, ma'am, I knew exactly where Will Bacon was headed. Had to get that drunk, no-count momma of his a bottle of whiskey before Mr. Jaber closed up at five. Didn't fool me none, not a bit."

"Wilma, just tell me what happened. Please! Do you know?"

"Sure she knows, Miss Emily!" Geneva hollered from the old stove. "Whole town knows by now what happened. Least ways, on this side of the track they knows."

"You don't, girl?" Wilma asked sarcastically as she tightened the green strap around her tiny waist. "Hell, and you're the smartest white person I know!"

"Go ahead and tell her, Wilma," Geneva said. "She sho' ain't gonna read it in the newspaper—that's for sure."

I could smell her coffee boiling on the stove, and I heard Wilma's mother chopping something on a wooden block. Then Geneva walked over to the table holding the biggest knife I had ever seen. "You want some wheat bread, Miss Emily? It's fresh, and we just churned some butter last night."

"No, thank you. I had some cereal before I left this morning."

"Suit yourself. Sure is good, though."

"As I was saying…" Wilma continued, but then she stopped when she heard her baby sister crying. "Nathan!" she hollered to one of her brothers in the back, "Get up and tend to Liza! Hurry it up—she's probably all wet! That darn boy'd sleep till nine if we'd let him." Then she leaned over and whispered to me so Geneva wouldn't hear her. "Let's get out of here and go talk. Too many ears and not enough walls; I'll just be a minute."

Wilma got dressed, and I had a cup of Geneva's strong black coffee.

I'll finish the story later when I write you more. There is a big meeting at City Hall tonight about the new Civil Defense plans. I must go.

Love,

Emily

October 16, 1941

Dear Harry:

I think Wilma wanted us to leave because she was embarrassed that I had seen where she lived, though she never would admit it. I doubt Geneva understood why I so abruptly left and went outside to the car after I finished my coffee, but I got the worst stomach cramps and became ill. I didn't want to alarm them, and I didn't tell Wilma when she finally came outside. It's nothing serious, and it's certainly too soon for me to begin having contractions, but the pain was so intense I almost fainted when I stood up to go outside. I don't drink coffee anymore, so I'm sure the cup Geneva fixed me probably upset my stomach. (Plus, I didn't sleep much after learning about Will's beating the night before.) But I don't want to bother you with my problems. There is much more important news I want to tell you, my love.

Wilma and I drove for several miles down the old levee road without either of us saying a word. She just stared out the window at a boat on the river with her chin resting in the palm of her hand. Finally, she said, "I've been watching that big tugboat push that coal barge upstream for about five minutes now, Emily. And you know what—it reminds me of me."

"Reminds you of you? What does that mean?"

"It's pushing hard but goin' nowhere fast. Just like

me."

I told Wilma to hush up because I was tired of hearing her feel sorry for herself.

"Just think about poor Will Bacon," I reminded her, "and that should help you—"

"Emily, you really don't get it, do you?"

"Get what?"

"Stop this car," she demanded. "Stop this car right now, girl! You and me needs to have a little talk. Damn, you're naïve! You're sure nice, but damn, you're naïve! If I was you, I'd start praying to that Saint Theresa friend of yours for some brains!"

I rolled down my window and waved the other Ford behind me to pass. Wilma rolled down her window and lit a Camel cigarette. Then she said, "Didn't your folks tell you *nothing* 'bout what happened to Will Bacon?"

I just looked at her and shook my head.

Then Wilma said, "You remember that old redneck in those dirty overalls at Jaber's Grocery that morning—the one who said something nasty to you, then watched us both like a cat?"

"That 'Mr. Scruggs' man?"

"Yes, that's him. Well, it was his son, Eddie, and two of his white trash cousins who beat up Will Bacon. You think that was just a coincidence or something?"

"I don't understand what you're getting at, Wilma."

"Of course you don't, Emily, 'cause you're thinking like a white person! Try thinking like a Negro for a while, and you might learn somethin', girl! 'Course it weren't no coincidence that Eddie Scruggs just happened to be there! Hell, his old man told them to be there at five o'clock and jump on Will, after he left!"

"But why would they do such a terrible thing?"

"Because he's a darn sissy, Emily, and everyone in town knows he ain't got no intentions of ever joining up to fight."

"But he says he's trying to get accepted to West—"

"Are you crazy? They'd never take someone like him! You're the only person I know who's foolish enough to buy that story."

"Well, I don't care if Will ever enlists. I don't think someone should have to fight if they don't want to. His mother needs him home, anyway."

"That mother of his? Hell, don't make me laugh! All that woman wants to do is sit on her big white fanny every day and get drunk with those other old cows she plays cards with. Momma cleans for one of 'em. She told me 'bout their card games."

"It's not Will's fault," I said, "and I think we ought to go visit him in the hospital this morning—see if he's okay."

But I could tell Wilma wasn't interested in visiting Will Bacon with me. She was quiet for a few moments, and then she said, "You know what your problem is, Emily Hodge?"

"Yes. I'm six months pregnant and not married."

"Well, in addition to that, you're too damn nice. Those Scruggs boys didn't beat Will Bacon just because he's a sissy—they jumped on him too 'cause he was seen with you and me."

I told Wilma I couldn't accept that. "Why would that matter?"

"'Cause all the white people in town say you like

black folks better than them—and that matters, honey, in a place like this. It matters a lot! And now a little sissy kid's done got his butt whipped because of it."

"You mean because of *me*—isn't that what you're trying to say, Wilma?"

She flicked her cigarette out the window. Then she said, "I mean because we're living in a place where no decent white girl like you should be hanging around with some n—— like me."

I looked at Wilma as hard as I possibly could—straight in her eyes, "Don't you *ever* call yourself that again—do you hear me!"

Wilma just looked out the window and stared at that same tugboat. Finally, she said, "We might as well go visit Will Bacon. I ain't got nothin' better to do. And no tellin' what kinda lies he might try to tell you up there if I ain't with you."

We drove to the hospital, and Wilma told me that Will Bacon had been buying whiskey for his mother from Mr. Jaber for some time now. Though I didn't understand why Mrs. Bacon couldn't buy her own alcohol to drink, Wilma explained that Will did practically everything for his mother since Mr. Bacon was killed in that hunting accident three years ago. I don't think I ever told you about that—it was such a strange thing, and supposedly it drove Mrs. Bacon to drink.

Mrs. Bacon had always been a "teetotaler Baptist," but she started drinking right after her husband's funeral and, according to Wilma, hasn't stopped since. Geneva told Wilma she overheard Mrs. Brandon say that Will's momma got drunk at a bridge game once and confided to one of her friends, "I do miss my husband, but I don't regret drinking. I should have started years ago."

I think that was easy for her to say. It's Will who's really suffered. He waits on his mother hand and foot. Does everything for her—brings home the groceries, cooks, cleans. I don't think there's any way Mrs. Bacon could stand for Will to leave her and go to West Point—even if it were true.

But in a strange way, I do feel sorry for Mrs. Bacon. I might as well tell you, everyone suspected Mr. Bacon actually killed himself out in the woods.

Supposedly, he had gone deer hunting alone on some of their property near Addison. The newspaper reported that he leaned his shotgun against a tree, but it fell and discharged and struck him in the face while he was sitting down to rest. But we never believed a word of it. Father used to play poker with Mr. Bacon every Wednesday night, and he's sure he committed suicide.

Father said Mr. Bacon was too experienced of a hunter to have ever done something that negligent. The story was, Mr. Bacon had taken some money from the Savings and Loan where he worked and had gotten caught, so that's why he killed himself. At his funeral, though, no one said a word about it. But I always liked Mr. Bacon. It's sad how some people's lives just end like that. They make one mistake and don't realize God forgives them anyway. Wilma said that's the problem. If people would just forgive themselves, like God does, Mrs. Bacon wouldn't be a drunk today.

But I think it's Will who was affected the most. I heard he almost dropped out of high school because he had to get a job to support his mother and himself. I guess Mr. Bacon didn't leave them much money. I always thought they had old money since they owned that big cotton plantation in Addison.

Mother said it wasn't worth much, though, since land up there was still going for Depression prices. And Mother heard the Savings and Loan sued Mr. Bacon's estate to collect what they claimed was missing. Nothing more was ever said about it. Mr. Bacon was from one of the oldest families in town, and Wilma said that was Will's problem, too damn much "blue blood" in his veins.

When we got to Will's room at the General Hospital, he had the sheet pulled up over his head. Wilma nearly screamed because she thought he was dead and said, "I ain't goin' 'round no dead person! I's scared of 'em!"

"I'm not dead, you foolish Negro!" Will Bacon said from underneath his sheet. "I just don't want you both to see me like this. I look—deformed."

"Pull down that sheet, Will Bacon, and let's get a good look at you," said Wilma. "You obviously ain't that bad off if you're talkin'."

Will had two black eyes, his nose was broken, and his top lip was swollen as big as a sausage. The nurse told us later that he also had a concussion and three bruised ribs. Seeing him like that, just lying there like a helpless little boy, I almost cried. But Will made a big joke about the whole affair and swore he'd tell us how he single-handedly defended himself against those three "sluggos" when he could talk better.

I could tell Wilma was uncomfortable the whole time we were there so we finally left, and I took her back home. I didn't see Wilma again for several days and don't think I wanted to. I didn't like that she was so unfeeling toward Will Bacon. Even if he is a sissy, it's not really his fault.

    Love,
    Emily

October 24, 1941

Dear Harry:

Mayor Burns announced at the Civil Defense meeting last week that we must begin preparations for the air-raid drills that will begin in December. Isn't that absolutely ridiculous? We're not even at war—and why would the Germans want to bomb Mississippi, much less Hamilton? Someone spoke up at the meeting and reminded us that the Japanese and the Italians are also fighting with Germany.

Old Mr. Swims, who's been to Japan several times, according to Father, told us the Japanese are a "determined people" and not to be trusted, so we had best be prepared. Mayor Burns then read the letter he received from Governor Johnson declaring Hamilton an "Auxiliary Base Town" since the National Guard is training here, so Father and the Board of Aldermen voted to have air-raid drills every Sunday, starting in two months. I think it's silly, but Father said Biloxi has already started. Our Civil Defense director, Mr. Kidd, has been on the coast this past week, learning how to conduct an air-raid drill, and Sharon Kidd told me after Mass on Sunday that everyone down there is serious about these drills. I guess that's easy to understand with a new Army base there now and Biloxi being on the Gulf Coast.

But it's pretty farfetched to believe some German

or Japanese airplane could ever bomb Hamilton. I mean no disrespect by this, my dear, but if the Yankees couldn't destroy Hamilton, Mississippi during the Civil War, then I don't think our present enemies can either.

All my love,
Emily

October 27, 1941

Dear Harry:

I was elated by the news in today's *Times Herald* that the unit from Camp Shelby will arrive this Friday! Will you be joining them, my love? Please write and let me know, for we have been apart now for much too long. This separation from you, however justified or deserved, has been my personal Hell.

How I long to see you, and not a night has passed when I haven't prayed you shall return. And when I dream at night, it is always of you.

We need to discuss what we will name our precious child and when the two of us can join you.

My prayer tonight is that I will see you soon.

Good night, my love.

Emily

P.S. Still, I await some news from you. Anything! But from dawn to dusk and dusk to dawn, I will continue to think only of you.

Emily

Newspaper clipping from the Hamilton Times Herald, *dated October 31, 1941, that was clipped to the back of Miss Emily's last letter to Harry:*

Troops from Camp Shelby, just south of Hattiesburg, began arriving today. As eagerly expected, a caravan of Army Air Corps trucks rolled into Hamilton at six-thirty this morning.

A crowd of about five hundred local citizens was on hand to greet them at Hargis Airport, where several units from the Mississippi National Guard have been stationed the past few weeks. The Army Air Corps unit from Camp Shelby has been sent to Hamilton to begin training the Guard troops. Captain Streete Wilder of Memphis, who is in charge of the Army Air Corps, said his unit plans to be in Hamilton for "five or six months" to fully complete their mission.

Local dignitaries on hand this morning to greet the caravan from Camp Shelby, as it rolled into town and proceeded north to the airport, included Mayor Elmo Burns and Aldermen Hodge, Jenkins, and Dombrowski. Mayor Burns officially welcomed the new troops to Hamilton and presented Captain Wilder the "Key to the City." The Hamilton High School band played "America the Beautiful" and "Dixie," while the crowd sang and cheered.

Two local men who had been training at Camp Shelby for the past several months have recently been accepted as pilots in the new Army Air Corps. Second Lieutenants Corey King of Hamilton and Harry Devening, a former Hamilton resident, were both expected to return here today to help train the National Guard. It was reported, however, that Lieutenant King is ill with the flu and that Lieutenant Harry Devening has been sent up north on special assignment.

November 14, 1941

My Dear Harry:

I am sorry I haven't written you these past two weeks. When I realized you weren't with the unit from Camp Shelby, I wanted to die. I think I could feel our little child stir inside my womb. Maybe, in some way, our baby sensed my grief and cried too.

I miss you terribly. Yet I can't even express how much I need to see you—to hold you and touch you again. I feel like I am all alone—adrift, as it were, on an ocean of despair. But I must press on—not just for my sake, but mainly for the sake of this precious child I want to bear for you.

Still, how I prayed you would return. I promised Saint Theresa I would name our child after her—should the baby be a girl—if she would only send you back to me. And how I begged God you would be with those troops when they came here two weeks ago! Wilma and I had driven out to Hargis Airport at six that morning to await your arrival. And I can't tell you how my heart jumped when I saw those first caravan headlights come over a hill down the road, headed our way. It was so crowded, my dear—you wouldn't have believed all the people who were there. When the high school band began playing, a cheer rose up from the crowd that was deafening. Members of the Rotary Club had already passed out small American flags, and it was a glorious sight to see everyone so excited. Even Will Bacon was there with his momma and some Negro man who was driving their car. They were parked on the side of the road across from us and several yards down, but I could see Will sitting in the back seat with dark glasses on and his arms folded across his chest. He didn't look like he wanted to be there at all, and I'm sure he was self-conscious about what happened a few weeks ago. (I'll have to write you more about that later.)

When the first Jeep arrived carrying Captain Wilder and the rest of his officers, I felt so special to be there. How I identified with every woman who has ever waited for the man she loves to return home. Isn't it strange how this scene never changes? It almost seemed like I was watching a movie of this and not really there. I seemed so detached from it all, as if I were some spirit hovering above while the people below cheered and waved their American flags.

Maybe I sensed you weren't there? Maybe I feared you were dead? Maybe still, God was preparing me (or punishing me?) for the inevitable shock that you had been transferred up North? When I didn't see you climb down from any of those trucks, my worst nightmare came true: you had not come back. I went home that morning and cried all day until I finally fell asleep in my bed.

Please write me, my love—
Emily

November 22, 1941

Dear Harry:

I got up early this morning and drove Mother's car back to the airport. Wilma couldn't go with me since she has finally found work, cleaning for Mrs. Geisenberger. I spoke to Mother about Wilma after I overheard Mrs. Geisenberger and Mother talking on the telephone about her maid dying. Cora Lee had been with the Geisenbergers for almost thirty years, and she raised both the Geisenberger boys and took care of old Mr. Geisenberger before he died. Cora Lee was such a fine Negro woman—a true Christian, if I've ever known one. I asked Mother, after she got off the phone, if Wilma could help Mrs. Geisenberger around the house, as she will always need a maid. Mother thought Wilma was a mite sassy for an older, Jewish lady like Eva Geisenberger, but I assured Mother that Wilma is a good cleaner and an honest Negro, and she really needs the money. Wilma wants to go to Tougaloo College in Jackson in two years and then become a teacher, so I encouraged her to start working now and save her money. I think I have told you before, but Wilma is so smart. It's a shame she had to be born in Hamilton, Mississippi. What a curse for an intelligent Negro girl like her. But if anyone can rise above their cruel circumstances, it is Wilma Watson.

I asked Will Bacon if he would accompany me to

the airport. It really isn't good these days for a lady to be driving alone with all these soldiers in town. But I'm sure no one would consider harming a woman who is seven months pregnant. Father reminded me that one can never be too careful. I dare say, though, that someone with my "notorious reputation," as Will Bacon quickly pointed out, is generally safe. And I do trust all our Catholic relatives in Heaven to look after and pray for us. I heard a nun say that in the third grade, and I have never forgotten it. That is such a wonderful and comforting thought in troubling times, don't you agree?

Will Bacon has mostly recovered from his wounds. And though he hasn't said, I suspect they were much worse than he let on. His face isn't swollen anymore, but his nose still doesn't look right. And I noticed he flinches in pain every time he inhales a cigarette. Wilma said his mouth must not have been hurt too badly because he still talks just as much. I think that Wilma, deep down inside, feels sorry for Will because he is such a misfit. Maybe she can relate to him, even though he's white, since he's as out of place here as she is. I don't know—maybe all *three* of us are out of place here in Hamilton?

Will asked me on the way to the airport, "So—Harry's not coming back, right?"

"Will Bacon, why are you always so nosy?"

"I'm only nosy with people I care about, Emily. As far as other people are concerned, I couldn't give a—"

"It would appear that way, for the time being."

"Time being? Don't you read the paper, dear? Seems like I recall it saying that Harry hightailed it back home. You know—up north, where all the Yankees live."

"That's only temporary," I informed him. "The article said Harry was on a 'special assignment.' "

" 'Special assignment'—right. Like I'm on a special assignment for the Klan. Don't make me laugh, Emily; it hurts my ribs. You know as well as I do that Lt. Harry Devening asked to be transferred so he wouldn't—"

"Shut your mouth, you little *thief*!" I yelled at him, and I regretted it as soon as I said it.

"Thief? Oh, come now, Emily, I may be a lot of nasty things, but a thief is certainly not one of them! And you should never believe *anything* you read in that rag of a newspaper."

"How dare you even *think* Harry didn't want to come back here! Who are you to be speaking of his intentions? You barely know him. And I don't think you're much of a man, Will Bacon—so there!"

"Oh, don't be so damn dramatic. And quit taking life so seriously. Look at me—I don't."

"You have no reason to because no one takes *you* seriously! Besides, you're still just a boy. What do you know about anything?"

" 'Boys' are fighting and dying every day, Miss Hodge—or don't you ever listen to the radio? And need I remind you that you're only twenty and a mere three years older than me? Though I must admit, you are— how should I say this—much more 'experienced' than yours truly."

Then I told him, "I don't know why I asked you to ride out here with me this morning, Will; I really don't."

"Well, probably because Wilma has finally got off her butt and found herself a job, and I don't have school on Saturday—don't you think? But I was hoping it was because we enjoy each other's company so much."

"Don't flatter yourself, Will Bacon. No one enjoys your company."

"Quite the contrary, my dear. I can assure you that I am held in the highest regard by the Scruggs family, who reside on a hog farm somewhere south of town. Hell, I made those rednecks famous! I mean, do you seriously think a palooka like Eddie Scruggs could have been written up in the paper if it hadn't been for me?"

I didn't respond to Will Bacon's nonsense after he said that. I began to feel slightly faint, but I just assumed it was from all the cigarettes Will had smoked since we left his house. So I asked him to roll down his passenger-side window because all the smoke was making me nauseous.

"As I was saying," he continued, "I have made Eddie Scruggs the hero he is today. Of course, he likes me—he *has* to! But that wretched father of his—God, I detest that man." Will got quiet for a few seconds. Then he added, "Harlan Scruggs killed a Negro boy once. Did you know that?"

"Will, I don't believe that story. I asked my father once if it were true, and he said—"

"Hell, yes, it's true! I don't care what *anyone* says. I know for a fact it's true because—"

"Because what? How do you know for a 'fact' that it's true?"

"Because Daddy knew Harlan Scruggs, and my daddy never lied to me. That's how!"

Then he said, "Daddy loaned Harlan Scruggs some money once from the Savings and Loan, so he invited Daddy to come hunt deer down at his place. Daddy really didn't like Mr. Scruggs—he was so common and all—but he loved a good hunting trip. I remember him telling Mother that the deer down there were the biggest in the county. So he went. And that night, Harlan Scruggs and some of his farmer friends got real drunk and started bragging how they had once lynched this Negro boy, just to watch him scream and kick. Then they took his body down and tossed kerosene on it and burned him up so nobody could identify him, and after that they went home like nothing had ever even happened.

" 'Just having a little fun with a n——,' Daddy said Harlan Scruggs bragged to him. Daddy never told anyone else that story but me."

"That's a horrible story, Will, and I don't believe one word of it. I don't mean any disrespect to your father, but I just can't believe anyone could do such an awful thing like that to another human being."

"Oh, my God, dear! What planet did you just come from? Are you for real? I would pinch you for asking such a silly question if you weren't seven months pregnant! Don't you know what's going on in the rest of the world? People are doing 'awful things'—just like that—to 'other human beings' all over Europe! My word, Emily—that damn Hitler's killing thousands of Jews every day! Whole towns of them! Those Nazi soldiers of his in those tacky black uniforms are lining up Jews like dominos and shooting them down. Damn, girl, you *better* believe it! And don't think it couldn't happen here! I used to listen to Father Charles Coughlin on the radio before he was silenced two years ago by that damn fool Roosevelt, and he used to claim that there are—"

"Will, if you feel so strongly about all this

injustice, then why don't you enlist like everyone else in your graduating class is doing and go fight Hitler?"

Will Bacon didn't answer. He pointed at the guard station about a hundred yards in front of us and said, "Slow this damn car down! They'll arrest you for speeding on a military base, you know? And don't be ridiculous, Emily. I'm trying to get accepted to West Point. You think I want to be some common private like that fellow up ahead with his hand raised in the air? I would rather die. Slow down, damn it—he's signaling to us or something!"

The young soldier stationed at the gate, who didn't look much older than Will, asked me for some kind of identification and why we were there. I told him I had come to meet with Captain Wilder to find out where you had been transferred. He asked who Will Bacon was and what business he was on. I had to lie and say Will was my younger brother and that our father, *Alderman* Hodge, had specifically wanted Will to accompany me since he was applying to West Point. I think the guard was impressed that my father was an alderman, so he wrote something down on a piece of paper and put it under my windshield wiper; then he let us pass. I don't think he believed Will Bacon was going to West Point because he rolled his eyes when I said that. After we drove onto the base, Will mumbled something about the young guard being a "damn Yankee," and then he said he only let us through because I was pregnant.

Hargis Airport looked so different—even from three weeks ago when Wilma and I were out there waiting for you. You can hardly tell it used to be a civilian airfield. It's now officially called "Hargis

Field," and they say in town it will soon be renamed after some general from the Great War, who I had never heard of. That doesn't surprise me, though, considering how fast everything and everyone is moving these days.

There must be two to three hundred soldiers out there now, and they were all busy when we arrived—walking around and carrying boxes or building a row of wooden barracks to stay in. I read in the newspaper that all the Guard recruits have moved from town and are sleeping in tents out there until the new barracks are finished. And I couldn't believe all the trucks, Jeeps, and airplanes they have out there. I don't remember seeing but two or three small planes when Wilma and I were there for the Welcome Ceremony. Will figures the Army probably flew the rest of them in one night while everyone was sleeping.

"Hell," he said, "if they'd flown in during the day, the whole town would have fainted from fear the Germans were invading us!"

There was a small, metal-framed building shaped like a loaf of bread that had obviously been recently built next to the terminal marked "Visitors," so I parked Mother's car in front and put on the hand brake. Will suggested he would stay in the car and watch my purse because someone might try to draft him if he got out. I know Will Bacon, though, and I knew he would go through my purse if I left it with him, so I took it with me and went inside the metal building by myself.

After I explained why I was there, I was escorted next door to Captain Streete Wilder's office inside the terminal by a nice corporal from Texas who said he knew you at Camp Shelby. "Mickey Waller," I believe he said was his name. Do you remember him, my love?

He's a big, cowboy-looking man about twenty years old, with a deep husky voice. He said he just slightly knew you since he was down at Shelby only three or four weeks before coming here. He was quite a gentleman, and he also said you were *the* best pilot in the camp. It thrilled me when he said that, but I could tell he was confused when I told him we weren't husband and wife.

"Little lady," he said, "Lieutenant Devening will be a famous pilot before this is all over. Yes, ma'am. Why, he'll probably make *general*!" Then he introduced me to Captain Wilder, who was seated behind a large oak desk, smoking a corncob pipe.

"What can I do for you, Miss Hodge?"

"*Emily* Hodge, sir," Corporal Waller offered on my behalf.

"That will be all, Corporal. Thank you. Now," Captain Wilder said to me with a faint smile and his pipe between his lips as he looked up from the papers on his desk, "what can I do for you, Miss Emily Hodge?"

He was younger than I imagined someone with the rank of captain to be. I figured he was about twenty-nine or maybe thirty, but his boyish eyes and smile could have easily passed him for twenty-five. I immediately suspected he smoked a pipe, instead of cigarettes or a cigar, to make him look more mature, and he reminded me of a boy I knew in high school who had to smoke a pipe in our senior play to try to look older, and all the pipe smoke caused him to faint on stage one night and vomit all over himself.

But when Captain Wilder spoke to me again, there was no mistaking his authority. "I understand that your father is Alderman Hodge in Hamilton?"

"Yes, sir, that's right."

"It must be nice to have a father who is important. So," he continued slowly, "I also understand you've driven out here today to inquire about Lieutenant Harry Devening—is that correct?"

"Yes, sir, that is correct. I was wondering if—"

"May I inquire, ma'am, as to *why* you're looking for Lieutenant Devening? Just what is your relationship to him?"

Will Bacon commented later that Captain Wilder must be blind to have asked such a stupid question like that, but I told the captain that you and I were "just friends."

"Friends," he said, somewhat puzzled. "What do you mean by 'just friends?' "

"Captain Wilder, with all due respect, sir, I don't really think that's any of your business."

He removed his wire-rim glasses and laid them down on the stack of papers in front of him on the desk. Then he took the pipe out of his mouth and exhaled a large puff of smoke. "You're right, Miss Hodge. That question was definitely none of my business. I apologize. May I assume then, Miss Hodge, that Lieutenant Harry Devening is the father of your child?"

I swallowed the lump in my throat before I answered him honestly, "I need to locate Harry, Captain Wilder. Can you please tell me where he's been transferred?"

Captain Wilder appeared genuinely moved by my question. He got up from his desk and walked past me to the front door on the other side of his office. He shut it and turned around; then he asked me to sit down. "It

David McCall Armstrong

isn't an order, Miss Hodge, but I would appreciate if you'd have a seat. You don't look very comfortable standing."

"Thank you, but I can't stay long. I have someone waiting out in the car."

"Your 'brother,' I believe?"

"Why, yes. Yes, that's right—my younger brother, Will."

Captain Wilder walked to the window behind his desk and peered through the Venetian blinds out into the parking lot between the terminal and the metal, bread-loaf building. "I take it that's your 'brother' out there in the black Edsel, smoking a cigarette. Is he old enough to be smoking?"

"Sir, I'm afraid my brother is incorrigible. He's already been rejected twice by West Point."

"Imagine that," he said, closing the blinds and returning to his wooden swivel chair. "How old is he, anyway? Has he enlisted yet?"

"Captain Wilder, sir, I'm really not here to talk about Will Ba...I mean, Will, my brother. I'm here to try to locate Lieutenant Devening."

He placed his arms on the desk and made a pyramid with his hands and tapped his fingers together several times as if he were in deep thought; then he finally said, "Lieutenant Devening is one of the finest pilots I've ever seen. I've never seen another flyer that could push an airplane to its maximum—like him. It's like he *is* the airplane—he becomes part of it! His maneuvers are excellent; his reflexes—amazing. When he first arrived at Camp Shelby, I flew with him one day in a two-seat trainer. He told me he used to fly barnstormers as a young teenager, somewhere up in

Indiana. Made pretty good money at it too, he claimed. I knew then he was good. Damn good. Too good to come up here with us to train a bunch of farm boys right out of high school who want to fly for the Mississippi National Guard. No, I'm afraid Harry Devening is much too valuable for that."

"So what are you saying then, Captain Wilder? Just where is Harry now?"

"I'm afraid I can't tell you that," he said abruptly. "He's been sent to a Special Alert Camp, somewhere off the East Coast, where he'll fly with the best pilots in the Army from across the country. That's all I know. I don't even know where the camp is, myself. I'd tell you if I did, 'cause Harry and I became good friends. But it's top secret. I'm sorry; that's all I can say. But I do have something for you. It's from Harry."

Then Captain Wilder opened his bottom right-hand drawer and removed a small tan envelope. He handed it across his desk to me, adding, "I'm sorry I haven't called you about this letter since we got here. Actually," he said, "I plain forgot. Everything's been so hectic. Harry asked me to find you after we arrived and give this to you."

Then he made another excuse why he didn't give the letter to my father when he met him at some city event two weeks ago, but I never heard what he said as I thanked him for his kindness and left the office—your precious letter held tight to my fast-beating heart.

Love,
Emily

November 23, 1941

Dear Harry:

I let Will Bacon drive Mother's car back to Hamilton while I clutched your letter to my breast. Maybe I was just imagining it, but the small, Army-looking envelope I held in my hand even smelled like you, my love.

"Why don't you quit smelling the damn thing and just read it?" Will Bacon demanded, about halfway home. I reminded Will for the third time that I had just kept him from being drafted into the Army, so he had better be nice to me.

"Besides," I told him, "I'm much too nervous to even *open* it—much less read it."

"Well, take the wheel, Emily, and I'll be glad to read every mushy word of it to you. It's the least I can do for your saving me from Uncle Sam."

"Not on your life," I told him emphatically. "Keep driving and watch where you're going. You almost hit that man driving those mules back there."

"There really should be a law against old Negroes and mules being on concrete public roads. I must speak to your father about that sometime."

I finally mustered the courage to open your letter. Bit by bit—first the left top corner, then the right. Slowly, I worked my right index finger down the flap, making sure not to tear the sacred seal. I could tell Will

74

Bacon was greatly agitated over all this, but I believe he was just as eager to hear from you as I was. He told me in the hospital, when Wilma and I went to visit him the second time, that he didn't understand why I hadn't heard a word from you in seven months. And though Will and I argue like sister and brother, I know he cares deeply for me—in his own way, that is.

"Open it, damn it! Or I'm stopping this car right this instant!" Will demanded.

I finally removed your letter from its envelope and immediately recognized your handwriting. What a truly wonderful sight that was! Even had it been only two words and nothing more, "Dear Emily" written by your own hand was the grandest thing I had ever seen!

(There was no end to this letter written by Miss Emily. But the following letter, still inside its envelope, from Camp Shelby, Mississippi, dated October 29, 1941, and simply addressed, "Miss Emily E. Hodge, Hamilton, Mississippi," was clipped to it.)

Camp Shelby, Mississippi
29 October 1941

Dear Emily—

I have missed you these past several months. We have been quite busy here at Camp Shelby, about six miles south of Hattiesburg. There is a guy here with me who I knew in Hamilton—Corey King—and we have both been accepted in the new Army Air Corps. A great honor! It is really exciting being a part of everything that is going on here. I am accepted in this place. There are guys here from all across the country. I even saw an old barnstormer buddy from Gary, Indiana in drill the other day! I don't have to constantly admit I am a "Yankee," because no one ever questions that at Camp Shelby. And I don't have to tell old ladies at church what my father does, back in Indiana, and then be embarrassed because he's a janitor, and I can't tell the truth. And most of all, no one cares or notices that I'm one-fourth Negro. I should have *never* told my secretary about that, but I didn't really think it mattered. What a fool I was! When she told my boss at the Steam Plant that I was a Negro, I knew my days with the Hamilton Power Company were numbered. Negroes, as you know, aren't allowed to do much more than cut grass for white people in the South—even a part-Negro, like me.

I had to leave Hamilton and a closed society that

would have never accepted someone like me. I do hope you understand. I tried to tell you that night when we drove out to Dillon Park for the last time. I knew it would be my final night with you, and I didn't want to hurt you. Emily, you're such a sweet girl, and you will make some man a wonderful wife one day.

I pray it is someone from *your* world, though, and not from mine. Though I do feel a great fondness for you, our worlds are too different for it to ever work between us.

You are a part of Hamilton and the old South, whether you like it or not, and I feel like I belong nowhere. It has always been hard being part Negro—even in Indiana! But I should have *never* told anyone about my heritage in Mississippi, even you. I would not hurt you for anything in the world. You were so good to me in Hamilton—so giving and tender to befriend me as you did—especially when I needed a good friend in that strange society of yours. And I couldn't bear knowing my dear friend, Emily Hodge, would be hurt in any way or thought harshly of because of me. So it was best that I leave and spare you any grief. It would have eventually happened, I assure you.

My greatest dream, as you know, has always been to be a pilot. I am so happy now, doing what I love most. Flying is a part of me; and if I have a soul, this is it.

I am someone else when I fly. Not Harry Devening—a "damn Yankee" from Indiana. Not a man who is part-Negro. I am a man inside a marvelous machine that can soar through the clouds! And if I should one day perish in pursuit of my dream, I will consider myself a lucky man. Please, Emily, always remember me that way.

I must end this letter now. I have been reassigned to what I have learned is a "Classified Special Alert Camp," somewhere off the East Coast. I cannot tell you how grateful I am and what this means to me. I leave tomorrow.

If I never see you again, dear sweet Emily Hodge, I am thankful for our brief time together.

I have asked Captain Streete Wilder to give this letter to you when our unit moves up to Hamilton in two days. I will not be joining them, but I trust he will do this for me. He is a fine pilot and a good friend. Always take care.

Harry C. Devening, Jr.

2nd Lt., Army Air Corps

P.S. By separate mailing, I am returning all of your letters, unopened. Please don't think of me as cold or unkind, for I do not feel that way toward you. I simply know it is best. I could never be a part of your life, or you of mine. Your future is in Hamilton where you belong, and mine is a dangerous one, at best, defending our country from a cruel enemy that will eventually strike. But when I finally leave to fight him in the skies, I will look down and always think of you.

Love,

Harry

"By all the castings down of His servants, God is glorified. For they are led to magnify Him when again He sets them on their feet, and even while prostrate in the dust their faith yields Him praise. They speak all the more sweetly of His faithfulness and are all the more firmly established in His love. Glory be to God for the Furnace, the Hammer and the Fire. Heaven shall be all the fuller of bliss because we have been filled with anguish here below, and the earth shall be better tilled because of our training in God's school of adversity."

~Charles H. Spurgeon

"And I know my Redeemer liveth—for He truly is a God of many deliverances."

~Emily E. Hodge
Hamilton, Miss.
November 25, 1941

December 7, 1941

Dear Harry:

We learned the horrible news today that the Empire of Japan has attacked some of our ships at a naval base called "Pearl Harbor" in Hawaii. I can't stand knowing so many of our fine young sailors have been killed by such a dastardly and cowardly act! Mother, Father, and I listened to President Roosevelt on the radio this evening, and he said he will ask the Congress tomorrow to declare war on Japan. We are all very frightened.

But this evil cannot go unchecked, and I thank God for brave men like you who are willing to fight for our country, no matter the cost. I am proud to have known you and loved you as I did, and I always will be.

I don't know if you will ever receive this letter because I don't know how to contact you. But should, one day, it happen to fall under your beautiful, kind eyes, I want you to understand what I am about to say and do.

In one of my first letters to you (that I will always save, my love!), I wrote to you that I was pregnant. I have always accepted full responsibility for this mistake, and I have never blamed you, for I am the one who wanted the relationship. These past eight months—living with the burden of my sin and guilt—have been so very, very hard. I have utterly embarrassed my parents and ruined my father's political career, and it has put a barrier between our love for one another that I pray can someday be healed.

Still, I go on. We have yet to truly discuss my pregnancy. My parents are so conservative that I don't think they could handle a frank discussion about their daughter's "improper ways." But I fully intend to approach them soon and tell them flatly what I did and how I love you, notwithstanding. And then I will tell them what I plan to do with this child of ours.

To hear from you that you might never return was to learn there is no God. And though I cannot accept that I may never see you again, I cannot forget my deep and enduring love for you.

Oh, Harry, my love for you is boundless and cries across the ocean of distance and differences that separate us!

But I must be realistic and think now of this precious life inside me. How I long to know if I will have a boy and if he will have your dear face. How I long to hold that little child and love him or her as I love you. What a wonderful blessing God has given me, despite the pain, hurt, and embarrassment of it all. And I am truly grateful to have shared myself for the first time with a man like you.

But I can't permit a child of yours to endure any of my shame. And it wouldn't be fair to you (for you suffered so much in Hamilton and may, yet, suffer more) to know your child is suffering here because he or she was born part-Negro and without a father. Those are two heavy burdens to impose on an innocent child.

So I have prayed to Saint Theresa and decided to put our baby up for adoption. Though he or she will never know either of us, somehow I know our child will always be loved.

And when I leave this cold world, before I meet my dear, sweet Lord and ask His forgiveness for my many sins, I will find that child (wherever he or she may be). If he is born a boy, I pray that Harry Hodge will grow into as fine a man as you. I will love you always.

Emily

December 10, 1941

Dear Harry:

There was a big rally at noon today in front of the Shane County Courthouse. Captain Streete Wilder stood and addressed the crowd over a loudspeaker, and he spoke for thirty minutes about the urgent need for young men to enlist, now that we are officially at war with Japan. I can see why he and you were such good friends. He seems like such a nice man, and he certainly is an impressive speaker.

He told us his orders were to call for 200 men from Hamilton, Shane County, and the surrounding areas. I'm sure, though, there were at least 300 men who enlisted today. I noticed several cars with Louisiana tags from across the river, and most of the men I saw went inside the courthouse and signed up before they went back home.

Mary Beth Dearing and her parents were there too, cheering with the rest of the crowd.

How brave I thought they were to come today, so soon after Danny's tragic death. Mr. and Mrs. Dearing were still wearing black arm bands in remembrance of Danny. When Captain Wilder then invited Mr. Dearing to come forward and address the crowd as the father of the first war hero from Hamilton, Mother and I both cried. Mr. Dearing spoke of his son's untimely death and how Danny's greatest love had always been his country, and he told us Danny's death will be in vain unless more of his young friends enlist and defend our country. Then everyone began cheering and applauding as Mr. Dearing left the podium, and even Mayor Burns was too choked up to speak.

Finally, the mayor said he regretted he was too old to defend America again as he had done in the Great War, but he urged the "brave young men of Hamilton" to follow in their fathers' footsteps and "join up today!" The high school band then struck up "The Star Spangled Banner," followed by "Dixie," and that was all it took for a line of men to start forming on the steps outside the courthouse and go inside to enlist.

Walking home that afternoon, Father told us that both the Army and Navy had set up tables inside the courthouse to handle the large crowd of men. Harry, you wouldn't have believed how many men registered today. We heard on the radio tonight that 384 men from Hamilton, Addison, Handsboro, and even from across the river in Somerset and Oakmont signed up to fight! It was truly a proud moment for our area.

Mr. Engle was the first person in line. Father said poor Mitch Engle is too old to be taken, but that he would do anything to get away from his nagging wife. I think Eddie Scruggs and his two cousins, Vernon and Nolan, were right behind Mr. Engle. I wondered if those "brave" farm boys realize they will be fighting a much tougher opponent now than sissy little Will Bacon.

I also heard on the radio this evening that Hamilton will have its first air raid drill this Sunday night, starting at six o'clock. All lights must be turned off at that time. Even the streetlights will be turned off at the

Steam Plant. We must pull down our shades and close the blinds, and the city is giving away black sheets to drape over all our windows. Personally, I think this is so silly and unnecessary, but it gives the old men in town something to do and an enemy to fight. Mayor Burns has placed Father in charge of the air raid monitors, and I haven't seen Father this happy in a very long time.

Love,
Emily

December 14, 1941

Dear Harry:

At early Mass this morning, Father Bruni gave a sermon on "Revenge" and why it is so wrong. What a peculiar subject I thought this was for him to choose, considering the recent atrocity the Japanese have committed, but I must admit it was one of the few thought-provoking sermons I have ever heard a Catholic priest deliver.

He said it was wrong to feel hatred in our heart toward another human being who has wronged us, and that Jesus said we must forgive our brother 490 times. I looked up the passage Father Bruni quoted in our old Catholic Bible when I got home, and he was right. Jesus *did* tell Saint Peter to forgive sinners "seven times seventy times!" I never knew that. What a tremendous challenge this is—one that I must go to Saint Theresa with in fervent prayer, for I am very guilty of this sin.

Several people left after Communion and didn't stay for the remainder of Mass. I believe I understand what Father Bruni was trying to say, and his sermon certainly gave me something else to pray about, but I don't think his sermon was appropriate. After Mass, I overheard several of the men refer to Father Bruni as a "damn disloyal Italian." Father's best friend, Frank Ford, leaned in the front window of our car as we were about to drive home and whispered, "That old priest should go back to Italy and fight for Adolph Hitler with the rest of his dago friends."

I have been writing this letter by candlelight since we are still under a Blackout until six o'clock tomorrow morning. I put an extra black sheet over all my bedroom windows so the "enemy" won't see my candle.

Emily

~

This prayer was stapled to the back of the letter:
Prayer of Saint Francis of Assisi

Dear God,
Make me an instrument of Thy peace:
Where there is hatred, let me sow love;
Where there is injury, pardon;
Where there is despair, hope;
Where there is doubt, faith;
Where there is darkness, light;
And where there is sadness, joy.
O Divine Master, grant that I may not so much seek to
    be consoled, as to console;
To be loved, as to love;
To be understood, as to understand.
For it is in giving that we receive;
It is in pardoning that we are pardoned;
And it is in dying that we are born to eternal life.
Amen.

E.E.H.
12-14-41

December 15, 1941

Dear Harry:

I had planned on discussing my "situation," as Mother refers to it, with my parents yesterday evening, but the Air Raid Drill and Blackout prevented our getting together to do so.

Father was busy all afternoon directing the Air Raid Monitors to their assigned streets to make sure everyone's lights were turned off. It was quite an undertaking, and far be it from me to spoil all the satisfaction he seems to be having. He takes things like this so seriously. (Wilma claims that's where I get my serious nature from.)

Father is also in charge of throwing the switch at the Steam Plant (on Mayor Burns' order, of course) to turn off all the streetlights in town. I sat on the porch with Mother in total darkness, and we talked about what great pleasure Father and Mayor Burns must have had doing this. "Like a couple of little boys at Christmas," Mother said, laughing, "out there drinking whiskey and throwing the 'big switch' to turn off all our streetlights so the Japanese won't bomb Hamilton too!" We both had a good laugh over that, and I think it was the first time Mother and I have laughed together in a long time.

I could just see Mayor Burns wearing his old uniform from the Great War that doesn't even fit him anymore. Mother said he probably was wearing that awful, plaid shirt he usually wears on Sunday afternoons when he works in their front yard around the corner. "He looks like a fat little elf," she laughed again, so he probably was quite a sight if he wore that shirt *and* his old Army coat! I can picture him out there commanding Father to "throw the switch and save the town" with a whiskey drink in his hand. God help us!

When Father finally got home last night, it was almost ten, and I could smell strong liquor on his breath. Mother gave him a head powder and then put him straight to bed.

I arose early this morning and prepared breakfast for the three of us. I scrambled some eggs, made toast and grits, and fried some bacon because Father loves it so much. There's nothing better than the smell of bacon frying in an iron skillet on a cold winter morning in December.

I could tell Father didn't feel well when he finally came down for breakfast. Mother and I were drinking juice when he walked into the kitchen and announced, still tying his bow tie, "The mayor told me last night that President Roosevelt is going to expand the draft. Guess we don't have to worry anymore about enough men enlisting to fight. They won't have a choice now."

I thought about Will Bacon when he said that. Will turned eighteen two weeks ago, and Father said all men between eighteen and sixty-four will now be eligible for "conscription." (Mother explained later that the term "conscription" meant getting a letter from Uncle Sam.)

So I telephoned Will Bacon's house immediately and asked his momma to have him call me as soon as he got home from school.

Love, Emily

December 16, 1941

Dear Harry:

Will Bacon drove straight to our house after school yesterday, and we sat on the screened porch since Mother won't allow anyone to smoke in her house. I got us both a cold Coke, and then I told him what Mayor Burns had told my father last night.

"Well, I'm not surprised," Will replied. "That's about par for that traitor Roosevelt."

"President Roosevelt is only doing what he thinks is best for the country, Will. Father doesn't care for him either, but he's not a 'traitor.'"

"President Roosevelt *is* a traitor, I tell you! Hell, he let the Japs attack us at Pearl Harbor while he was drinking gin with their damn ambassador! It's true!"

"You think you know everything, don't you?"

Then Will crushed out his cigarette in the ashtray and said, "No, Emily Hodge, I don't know 'everything,' but I do know this—that war-happy president of yours has just signed my death warrant."

"That's ridiculous, Will. Why would you say something like that?"

"Simple. Because it's true. Do you really think someone like me could survive being drafted, given a rifle, and told to 'shoot or be shot?' Hell, I may as well shoot myself first and save our government some time and money! Look, Emily, I couldn't even stand to go hunting with my daddy. Do you know I've never even fired a gun? God, I don't even know how to *load* one! I'm probably the only white guy in the whole damn state of Mississippi who's never killed a deer!"

"I seriously doubt that," I tried to reassure him.

Will lit another Lucky Strike, took a few drags, and said, "Listen, Emily, I'm serious now. You've got to help me."

"Sure, I'll help you, Will. What do you mean?"

"Promise me."

"Promise you what?"

"Promise me you'll swear that I'm the father of your child so maybe I can claim some sort of exemption and not have to go overseas and fight."

"You really are a cad, Will Bacon! Besides, no one in Hamilton would possibly believe something ridiculous like that."

"Maybe if I never opened my mail or moved Momma and me to an undisclosed address somewhere?"

"Really, Will," I interrupted his fantasy, "what are you going to do?"

"I don't know, Emily. I just don't know. You know what's strange about this, though?"

"*Everything* is strange about these days we're living in, Will. What is there that's *not* strange about it all?"

"No, that's not what I'm talking about. Listen, I had the weirdest dream last night. I dreamed I was walking through this huge field, and, all of a sudden, I saw my daddy sitting on an old tree stump up ahead, with his double-barrel shotgun resting across his lap— just staring out in the distance at something. Then the largest, most beautiful deer you can imagine, with this huge rack of antlers, came running across the field in front of Daddy. Daddy jumped up, raised his shotgun, and pulled both hammers back to fire. Then the deer just stopped and looked at me, like it was pleading with me to beg him not to kill it. I ran toward Daddy and started crying and begging him, 'Please don't kill that deer! Please don't kill that beautiful deer! It doesn't want to die; it just wants to *live*! Please, Daddy, please…'

"Then he lowered his shotgun, slowly turned around, and looked at me, but it wasn't Daddy anymore; it was old man Harlan Scruggs. That's when I woke up. What do you think that dream means, Emily?"

"I don't know, Will. I know you must have been terribly hurt by your father's death, but I don't think it's a good idea to dwell on such things."

"It means I'm responsible for my daddy's death, Emily—that's what it means! Hell, I've always known that! Daddy killed himself because he had a sissy son like me who's afraid to kill a deer! Who doesn't even know how to load a gun, much less shoot one!

"So tell me, Emily, or maybe you should pray about this to your Saint Theresa—you and her seem to be so close—how am I going to shoot another human being when I can't even shoot a damn deer?"

I didn't know how to answer Will Bacon. He had tears in his eyes when he asked me that, and I had never seen him so upset like this before. I felt so sorry for him, sitting on our front porch yesterday afternoon. What could I have possibly said to him or to any young man who feels the same way Will does? And I'm sure there're thousands of young men who are just as afraid.

I never realized before, but Will Bacon has no business in a town like this, either. He is so out of place here with everything and everybody. He has no friends (other than Wilma and me) that I am aware of. I regard him as a little brother and believe he looks up to me as an older sister since he has no one else in the world, other than an alcoholic momma who takes advantage of his sweetness. I do worry about him. (And if he doesn't gain some weight, I'm afraid he'll never find *anyone*.)

I finally heard the full story about what happened at Jaber's Grocery when Will got beat up by Eddie Scruggs and his cousins in October. I don't recall if I ever told you what really happened, but Genevieve Brandon wrote me a note a month or so ago and filled me in on all the details. Frankly, her letter confirmed what Will Bacon finally confided to me, but Will can be such a liar that you never know when to believe him.

Genevieve wrote to inquire how I was feeling, and then she began to write about Will Bacon. (Stephen, her husband, handled Mr. Bacon's estate—their families are distantly related.) This is what Genny wrote to me:

"Stephen, who also sends his fondest regards, came home and told me young Will Bacon visited his law office today to discuss the incident at Jaber's grocery two weeks ago. Stephen commented that Will looked like he had been kicked by a mule, so he inquired how he was feeling. Will said his ribs and his pride were still bruised, but his face was finally healing. Then Will told Stephen the truth about what happened.

"It seems Will Bacon had been to Mr. Jaber's store earlier that morning, buying cigarettes and bragging about going to West Point next fall. An old farmer from south Shane County named Harlan Scruggs, who I'm sure you've never heard of, Emily, was in there also and asked Will Bacon why he didn't enlist like all the other boys. Will then informed Mr. Scruggs that only a fool with no future would voluntarily join the Army! Mr. Harlan Scruggs then called Will a sissy little momma's boy, so Will left. But Stephen said he knows for a fact Will Bacon had come there with a Negro girl, and he thinks that infuriated Mr. Scruggs even further.

"The mistake Will Bacon made was telling old Mr. Jaber, in front of Harlan Scruggs, that he would be back that afternoon by five o'clock to purchase some 'medicine' for his momma. But everyone in town knows Mrs. Bacon's medicine is Red Crow whiskey. So Harlan Scruggs came back with his son, Edward, and two of his cousins, and they waited outside for Will to show up.

"Stephen said Will Bacon had no money with him when he came back to purchase the whiskey for his momma, but he promised he would return on Monday after school and pay Mr. Jaber then. Will swore this was the truth, and Stephen said Alfred Jaber really can't hear well, so that probably is what transpired. In any event, Mr. Jaber felt like Will had been punished enough so he never pressed charges, especially since he got his bottle of whiskey back. You know how those Arabs are, Emily—not much different than Jews!

"So that whole matter was totally unrelated to Edward Scruggs and his two cousins apprehending Will outside the store. They were there, at Mr. Scruggs' request, merely to teach Will Bacon a lesson to *quit being such a liar*! After all, everyone knows about Will Bacon's father embezzling all that money from the

Savings and Loan, and West Point would *never* accept the son of a man like that! I just thought you should know the truth.

"Call me sometime, Emily, and maybe we can visit on the telephone or go have a Coke."

That night, I officially added Will Bacon to my prayer list. He was so flippant and nonchalant about it all when he left that I knew he must be hurting terribly inside. I would give anything to be able to help him right now, but I know that I can't. How I regret this.

Love,
Emily

December 20, 1941

Dear Harry:

I don't know why, but I have been thinking today about when you left Hamilton for Camp Shelby. You got such an early start. It seems like such a long time ago now; so much has happened since you left. And if anyone had told me that morning when I hugged you goodbye that it might be our final kiss, I would surely have died. It is a moment I shall cherish in my heart forever.

I called Stephen Brandon after lunch and asked him if he would handle our child's adoption. Dr. Ernst told me last week, when I went in for a checkup, that everything was fine. Our baby has grown so much, and I am quite huge now. I fear you would hardly recognize me, for I have gained so much weight. Dr. Ernst is convinced I will carry this child to full term next month, but Geneva, who is an experienced midwife, called him an "old quack." She claims to know more about birthing babies than all the doctors in Hamilton! She thinks I will give birth two weeks earlier than Dr. Ernst predicts, and she also thinks it will be a little boy! How happy this made me to hear her say that, though I am none too sure how Geneva came to this conclusion. Wilma swears her momma "ain't never wrong 'bout babies." Then she added, "She ain't much on picking men, but she knows 'bout babies. So if Momma tells you it's a boy, you might as well go buy him some pants."

Geneva claims she can predict the sex of a child merely from feeling how low the baby sits in the womb! Have you ever heard of such? Sometimes Negroes say the strangest things, and they're so superstitious. But I don't know what I would do without Wilma and her momma—they have both been so good to me. (And I pray Geneva's sex prediction is right!)

But it occurred to me that it really doesn't matter if our child is a boy or a little girl. I only ask God that our child be healthy and a true blessing to some young couple who can't have children of their own.

Stephen Brandon said he hunts with another lawyer from Jackson who knows a couple who've been looking for a child to adopt. God has answered my prayer! All my love—

Emily

December 21, 1941

Dear Harry:

I finally told my parents this evening, immediately after dinner, that I had decided to put our child up for adoption.

At first my father didn't say a word. Then he got up from his chair and went over and turned off the program we had been listening to on the radio. He looked over at Mother sitting on the couch and said, rather coldly, "Your mother and I had already decided that this would be the proper thing to do. These are very difficult times, Emily, and we only want what's best for you."

"I don't mean to sound impudent, Father, for I do know what an embarrassment I have been to you both, but—"

"Emily, please," Mother interrupted, "it's much too late to—"

"No, Mother, let me finish; this needs to be said. You sound more concerned, Father, with your reputation than you do with the welfare of this child I'm about to bear."

"That's not fair, Emily!" Mother shouted. "How dare you say that to your father! After everything you've put us through these past eight months! Not many parents in this town would have supported a daughter who went out and did what you did. Have you once, just once, considered *our* feelings throughout this whole affair?"

"What do you mean by 'support,' Mother? Just exactly how have you and Father supported me?"

"By giving you a roof over your head and three meals a day—that's how! By not sending you away to some…'facility' where they could have done something about your situation. *That's* how we've supported you! Do you not understand this?"

"I see. You mean you would have preferred I went off somewhere and had this baby aborted? Is that really what you're telling me, Mother? How convenient that would have been for you both."

Father came and sat down next to me on the sofa. He put his hand on mine and said, "Emily, this has been very trying for all three of us. I don't want you to think for one moment that we don't care about you and your—"

"Oh, don't patronize me, Father—please! I'm not some little girl anymore you can manipulate like one of your voters at re-election time! Really. You should have more respect for me than that!"

"Respect for *you*?" Mother exclaimed. "What respect have you shown for *us*? You totally ruined your father's chances of running for mayor against that little idiot around the corner! Don't dare talk to me about 'respect' for you!"

"So that's it, isn't it, Mother? That's what this whole damn thing is all about—politics and your precious reputation in this town?"

"Emily," Father said, "please don't use curse words in our house. I will not allow it."

"Can you blame her, Avery? I mean, look who

she's been hanging around with the past eight months—a Negro and a *thief* who's too *sissy* to fight for his country! Oh, and let's certainly not forget the father of our soon-to-be grandchild—what was his name again, dear? 'Harry,' I believe? Yes, that's it. 'Harry Devening'—a Yankee who's also part Negro! No wonder she curses, Avery. Really, I'm surprised she hasn't taken up smoking and drinking yet!"

I could not listen to any more of this cruel talk from my own mother. I swear I will never forget what she said, for as long as I live.

"Dear Lord," I prayed that night after I said a Rosary in my rocking chair, "please forgive me for how I have hurt and humiliated my parents. How best it would have been had You taken me home to Heaven after Harry left. I could have spared my parents from the shame of this mistake, and I would now be free of my guilt."

After I crawled into bed and turned off the table lamp, I heard my Father crying in the bathroom down the hall. That was something I had never heard him do before.

Emily

December 23, 1941

Dear Harry:

I saw Captain Wilder at Lea's Drugstore in town today buying some tooth powder, and he acted so cordial to me that I was somewhat taken back. I guess it surprised me that he recognized me, but Wilma, who was waiting for me out in the car, was quick to point out that "the Army man probably doesn't see a lot of pregnant women in town so as to get confused."

I believe I told you how nice I think Captain Wilder is. And knowing he is a good friend of yours makes him even more special to me. If I may say so, any young woman in Hamilton would be lucky to land such a fine man as him.

I was curious why he was in town since I thought the Army had its own PX out at Hargis Field. When I asked him why he had come to town to buy some tooth powder, he replied, "Are you always this nosy, Miss Hodge?"

"Oh, Captain Wilder," I said. "Please forgive me. I didn't mean to be nosy. I just thought the Army had—"

"Actually, I came into town this morning for a meeting with Mayor Burns and your father about the new Air Alert Siren we're installing on top of City Hall. Have you seen the work our men have done? We also used some local folks in town and a local engineer to help."

"Yes. I was by City Hall before lunch, and I saw some of them on top of the building. You know, one man almost fell off?"

"No, not really," Captain Wilder leaned over and whispered in my ear. "But I overheard that rumor too—in here, just a few minutes before you walked in. Some little old lady with the bluest hair I've ever seen was telling the druggist that 'a new recruit just leaped to his death from the top of City Hall!' Then she asked him—no, let me rephrase that—she *demanded* of Mr. Lea, 'Just what do you reckon those soldiers are doing up there, Calvin Lea?' Seems to me Hamilton enjoys false rumors just as much as my hometown of Memphis does, big city or not."

We both had a chuckle about that because it certainly is true. Then he added, "But I came here to buy some black-cherry pipe tobacco. That stuff they sell at the PX is terrible, and it really stains my teeth."

(I personally think that Captain Wilder has beautiful white teeth, but far be it from me to ever say something so forward to a stranger.)

Back in the car, Wilma wanted to know who that "handsome Army man" was I was talking to and what we had been talking about.

"That was Captain Streete Wilder, Wilma," I reminded her. "Don't you remember seeing him last month when we went out to greet the troops? He's in charge out at Hargis Field now."

Wilma said, "Hell, girl, all white men in uniforms looks the same to me. 'Specially from a distance and without my lookin' glasses on my head."

I am happy Wilma is finally working. Although she's a Jew, Mrs. Geisenberger is such a good Christian lady. Her two sons are both doctors now—somewhere up north, and Wilma told me Mrs. Geisenberger said that Aaron, her youngest son, has just joined the Navy. I'm afraid our armed forces will probably need a lot of doctors from what I understand, so I'm very proud of Dr. Aaron Geisenberger for enlisting.

Wilma told me Mrs. Geisenberger is so good to her—she treats Wilma like a real person instead of some young Negro maid. Although she's a member of the Old South Garden Club here, as my mother is also, I don't think Mrs. Geisenberger has ever been accepted by those other ladies. Thinking about Mrs. Geisenberger, I understand now what you meant in your letter about never being accepted because you're different and not from here. Mrs. Geisenberger is Jewish and originally from Pennsylvania. And though she's been here now over thirty years, according to Wilma, she's still not "recognized" by the old Hamilton families. What a sad indictment on a community this is.

Love,

Emily

P.S. I forgot to mention that Captain Wilder did the strangest thing before I left the drugstore today. He squeezed my left hand so tenderly and said, "Merry Christmas, Emily." I thought that was rather forward for a man who doesn't even know me. Don't you?

December 30, 1941

Dear Harry:

I certainly hope Wilma doesn't persist in her conviction to quit her job with Mrs. Geisenberger! I just found out this afternoon and am totally put out with her! I simply don't understand why she would not want to work anymore for a caring, generous lady like Eva Geisenberger. It is beyond belief. Plus, after all Mother and I did to help her get that job—and I told Wilma so!

Wilma told me back, "Emily Hodge, I can't take care of Mrs. Geisenberger and you and your baby at the same time—so I just up and quit. And that's that. Ain't no point in tryin' to talk me out of it, neither!"

I haven't told Wilma yet that I have decided to put our child up for adoption. I don't know how she will take the news, especially now that this has happened. Wilma's quitting dear Mrs. Geisenberger has totally dampened my holiday spirit!

Love,
Emily

January 2, 1942

Dear Harry:

I am so excited and grateful to God for the splendid news I have just received this new year: Genevieve Brandon called and said Stephen has located a couple in Jackson who want to adopt our baby! Genny asked to give me the good news herself, and Stephen said the couple is thrilled to have finally found a baby to adopt. He said they had been looking for over two years.

Though I would like to know who this couple is and something about them, Stephen said it is best for everyone concerned that we never meet. They also do not know who I am, and Stephen told Genevieve to assure me that, by law, this must be the case. It all seems so secretive to give our child to two total strangers, but I am thankful there is someone out there who wants our baby. Genny also told me this is an "older couple" and that the father has a good job with a factory in Jackson, so that made me feel better. Supposedly, his wife has had three miscarriages, and their doctor advised that they could never have children. I view this as God having answered *two* prayers!

We haven't worked out all the details yet. Genny said Stephen wants to meet with me at nine o'clock on Monday morning to discuss when the adoptive parents can "acquire" the child. They also have insisted to pay for all the expense of my delivery. I didn't want to accept such a generous offer from them, but Stephen advised that this is an "ordinary and customary expense" of adoption that they should bear. I finally agreed. I also wondered about the adoptive father's draft status, but Genny told me not to fret about that.

I guess it's all set, then. Harry, I have prayed this would happen for so long that I can't believe it's true! I know now that God does answer prayers, and I am so grateful to Saint Theresa for her intervention on my behalf.

I can only pray now that our little child (and I do believe it's a boy, as Geneva claims) will be loved, and that he will have a better life than I could ever provide. And though I will always miss not being able to care for and love our son, I am more concerned that he never knows the shame and agony of rejection. And how a boy needs a father—this I could never give him. Away from here—from me—our son will have a happy and normal life. And if I never meet our precious boy and behold his dear sweet face in this life, we will all be together one fine day in Heaven.

Love,
Emily

January 5, 1942

Dear Harry:

I don't know what to do about Wilma. She still will not consent to go back to work for Mrs. Geisenberger! Mrs. Geisenberger has begged her twice to come back—even for 50 cents more a day, but Wilma is so stubborn. She claims the money has nothing to do with it. (Maybe she *is* "plain lazy," like Will Bacon claims?)

And now we're hardly speaking after I told her I was putting our child up for adoption. The way Wilma reacted, you would think this baby was hers!

Wilma said, "It ain't natural to give your own child away—and it sho' ain't Christian, neither. Momma says God's gonna punish you for doin' that."

I told her flat out, "I don't care what your momma thinks or says. She may be a midwife, but it's none of her business. For that matter, it's none of *your* business, either!"

"The hell it ain't! Who you think been your best friend, girl, these past eight-and-a-half months? Huh? It sho' ain't been that snooty little Genny Brandon with all that blonde hair of hers. Looks like ole rag-doll hair, anyway."

"Why are you so upset about this, Wilma? Yes, you have been my best friend, and I am very grateful for that. Fact is, you've been my *only* friend since Harry left. But why should you care what I do with my baby?

This child inside me is mine—not yours! Don't you understand that I'm only doing what's best for—"

"You're only doing what's best for *you*, Emily. You're only doing what's best for you. Just like those parents of yours—and just like every other white person I've ever known. Y'all only think of yourselves."

"Wait a minute, Wilma. I'm not going to let you get by with saying that; that's not fair. I've also been your friend too, you know? If I'd been thinking only of myself, like you claim, you think I'd be seen going all over town with a—"

"A what, Miss Emily? A n——?" Then she thought a second before she said, "You know, girl, you're no damn different than all the rest, when you get right down to it. You're just a little slower to catch on, that's all. I've got to go. Momma's birthing a baby 'cross the river today, and she needs me. Goodbye, Miss Emily."

Harry, I don't know what to think of what Wilma said. What did she mean by I'm "no different" than the rest of these people here? God knows, if anyone is different—it's me!

How I wish I *weren't* different! What a great trial by fire my parents and I would have been spared. Not different? I am utterly floored by this. No words have ever stung me or cut me to the quick more than those Wilma said to me today.

So now I am left all alone, without you and without, it seems, my dear friend Wilma. I have never felt so abandoned in all my life.

But maybe this is my punishment? Maybe this is what some folks call "the wrath of God"?

I really don't believe that, though. I don't know if

I've told you before, but I believe now in a God of forgiveness and love—not in a God of revenge. Father Bruni was right.

Emily

January 8, 1942

My Dear Harry:

I am confined now to staying home and resting on the couch. Dr. Ernst has forbidden me to drive Mother's car anymore, and I am much too heavy to walk. So I occupy myself by reading and listening to programs on the radio. I am sick and tired of all the war news that's on. It seems this is all they have to report now.

How selfish of me to feel this way. With all the thousands of people being killed every day, I shouldn't be complaining. I am ashamed of myself.

I ramble so much in these letters to you. My writing is terrible, I know, but there is always so much I want to tell you—to share with you. It finally occurred to me, though, I never ask about you. Please forgive me for this, my dear. How I would cherish another letter from you—anything—just to let me know you are safe and still alive.

I thought about driving again out to Hargis Field to speak to Captain Wilder about my dilemma. Surely he knows where you are? But that is totally out of the question, I know. Maybe I should call him? Maybe God will grant me one more request and allow Captain Wilder to come visit me? Yes, I will call him tomorrow, and I'll ask him if he would do me the greatest favor in the world.

Emily

January 9, 1942

Dear Harry:

I spoke with Captain Wilder this morning, and he advised that he'll stop by my house tomorrow afternoon, promptly at three o'clock. This is wonderful news and a definite sign from God! I know this is going to work. I'll explain in my next letter. I must get some rest now; I am not feeling too well this afternoon.

Love,
Emily

January 10, 1942

Dear Harry:

Mother said I am much too forward, inviting a total stranger from the Army into our house in broad daylight. How ridiculous. I politely reminded her that Captain Streete Wilder is the Commander out at Hargis Field, so we should be honored that he would take time to pay a civilian a visit. I think her main concern, though, is what the neighbors will think. I couldn't care less what they think. I feel sure their opinions of me are none too high, as is.

When Captain Wilder comes here this afternoon, I will ask him to please locate you and, somehow, get my new letters to you. They are all neatly packed in a small sewing box I have wrapped with brown paper and sealed with your name on the outside.

I know Captain Wilder will do this for me; after all, he is your friend.

Must get some cleaning done now so I can be ready before he gets here at three o'clock.

I love you,
Emily

Thursday, 1/15/1942

My Dear Emily,

I'm writing because I didn't want to come by and get all misty-eyed and everything and make a total fool of myself—especially right before you go into labor. (God, that sounds like a dreadful word—"labor"—ugh!)

Anyway, I just wanted you to know I have enlisted in the Navy. Me, a Seaman—can you believe it? I figured it was the "honorable" thing to do, and it damn sure beats getting drafted by the Army! So I went down to the courthouse and signed up yesterday. It's over and done with, and that's that.

I'm sure I shocked the hell out of everyone who was in there. I told them *emphatically* that my one condition in joining was that I *must* get a top bunk! You should have seen the look on that Navy guy's face when I said that—thought I'd fall to the floor laughing!

Anyway, I couldn't let Eddie Scruggs and his two Army cousins get all the glory from defending our country. So what the heck—I'm going to do my part too!

Momma is pretty upset with what I've done. I don't know how she'll get along without me. She drank heavily last night and passed out on the couch. Poor thing must have slept there all night, I guess. Seems like I can't ever please my parents, you know. Hell, I thought the woman would be proud that her "sissy" son is finally acting like a man.

I had another dream about Daddy last night. Really scared me this time. I think, though, that he would be proud of me now. God, I wish he were still alive, Emily! I really loved that man.

I'm sorry I won't be with you when you have your baby. Probably best, though—I'd most likely faint or say something stupid. I assume Wilma and that uppity midwife mother of hers will take good care of you after the deed is done. Be sure to tell them that Seaman First-Class Bacon sends his most cordial regards.

Dear sweet Emily, you've been like a sister to me this past year. I only wish I could stay here longer and be with you and your child. I'm serious now—for once in my life. I really mean this: I love you and always have. But I've got to leave Hamilton. Who knows, I might even come back from the Navy as an officer. Lord, help me, though.

Don't know when I'll get back to Hamilton. I'm taking a bus down to New Orleans in the morning to catch a train to Pensacola, Florida, where I'll be stationed.

But don't worry, Miss Emily Hodge, for you shall see me again.

Love you always,
William S. Bacon, III
Seaman First-Class
Uncle Sam's Navy

The following letter was in a different envelope with no return address. The envelope was postmarked Gary, Indiana and dated May 4, 1944. It was addressed to Emily Hodge, Hamilton, Mississippi.

18 January 1942

Dear Lt. Devening,

How are you, buddy? Guess they're treating you okay up there? You lucky guy! I'm sending this letter in hopes they can locate you. The "Ole Man" never tells us low-class fly boys *anything*!

Have they let you get behind the wheel yet of one of those new Boeing B-17s that Top Brass is so high on? I hear tell they call the damn thing a "Flying Fortress." I'm not surprised. One of my junior officers brought me a picture of one last week—mighty, mighty impressive!

Not much going on here at Hargis Field. Most of the time spent yelling at a bunch of kids in the National Guard who think they want to be pilots, like us. Hell, what do they know about war? For that matter, what do *we* know about it?

Are you doing all right, pal—on this secret mission of yours? Damn sure wish I was with you doing something important instead of training a bunch of new recruits. But you're the best, Harry—no denying that.

By the way, I went to see Emily Hodge last Saturday, and she asked me to get a box of her letters to you. If this one makes it, wire me your address and I'll stick them on the next train headed your way. Better yet, pal, why don't you write and let me know what being a *real* pilot is all about! Take care—

Captain Streete Wilder
U.S. Army Air Corps
Hargis Air Field
Hamilton, Miss.

P.S. Almost forgot. Congratulations on becoming a new papa! I heard in town this morning that your Emily gave birth to a little boy, early this morning. So how come you didn't mention this down at Camp Shelby? You devil, you!

Streete

This telegram followed the previous letter:

24 JANUARY 1942
CAPTAIN STREETE WILDER
HARGIS AIR FIELD
HAMILTON, MISSISSIPPI
YOUR LETTER RECEIVED TODAY STOP
MANY THANKS STOP IN NEED OF A FAVOR
STOP PLEASE DELIVER FORTHCOMING LETTER
TO EMILY HODGE ASAP STOP LEAVING
TOMORROW ON SHIP FOR ENGLAND STOP
WILL CONTACT YOU WITH ADDRESS LATER
STOP
HARRY DEVENING, JR.
1ST LIEUTENANT
U.S. ARMY AIR CORPS
WARWICK, RHODE ISLAND

David McCall Armstrong

The next item was the following obituary from the Hamilton Times Herald, *dated January 21, 1942:*

Graveside services were held today for baby Harold Hodge of Hamilton, who was born at the General Hospital on Sunday, January 18, at 2:40 in the morning. According to Dr. Raymond Ernst, family physician and friend, the infant developed heart and lung complications late Sunday evening and died early the following morning. Father Anthony Bruni of St. Ann's Cathedral conducted a private Catholic service at the family plot in the Hamilton City Cemetery.

The mother of the baby boy is Miss Emily Edna Hodge of Hamilton. Maternal grandparents are Alderman and Mrs. Avery Hodge, longtime Hamilton residents. The mother requests that no flowers be sent, but memorial donations may be made to the War Relief Fund at the First Hamilton Bank. Family friends may begin paying their respects tomorrow afternoon.

24 January 1942
Warwick, Rhode Island

My Dear Son—

At the time of this writing, you are only a few days old, and how I would love to hold you in my arms and just look at you. But I am going away tomorrow and about to miss the best part of your life. Someday I hope to make up for this lost time, and more. I know your coming into this world has brought a lot of joy and happiness to your mother, though.

Please tell her I understand now why she wrote me all those letters while I was still in Mississippi at Camp Shelby. Tell her, too, I was afraid to open them and read them because I knew what they would say. I had already heard she was pregnant with you, but I wasn't man enough to contact her and assume my responsibility.

But I don't want to go into all that now. How can I expect either of you to understand why I left and didn't stay to do the honorable thing? Maybe one day, when you are older, it will make better sense. Hopefully, it will to me then too.

In the event something happens to me while engaged in this present conflict, there is only one request I ask of you: Take good care of your mother and look after her. Respect her, and above all, carry out her wishes with obedience—whether you think it right or wrong. She is a very fine and beautiful woman, with love and intelligence far superior to mine. Be a friend to her; feel free to converse with her at any time on any subject, and you will be a man everyone will respect. Be intelligent, alert, and lead a good Christian life. There is nothing more important than this.

To be a strong man with leadership qualities, you must possess both a strong mind and a strong body—build both while you are young. Never put off until tomorrow what you can do today, for tomorrow may never come. Take whatever happens and get the most out of life as each day passes.

I trust when you are old enough to read this letter, you won't consider it a lecture but something to possess as life goes on. It would be foolish on my part, or anyone else's, to try to map your life for you. We only tell you those things which are right and honorable and hope you will build your life around them. We learn from experience and not by what someone tells us, and sometimes this is costly.

Youth is a great thing, and you only possess it once, so take advantage of it. I expect you to be a real boy, mischievous and fun-loving. As you grow older, you will realize, and only you, just what your youth meant to you, the things you did and accomplished. The older you get, the more you respect intelligence, health, and happiness.

The only request I have of God is to see my son and his mother again, and maybe someday the three of us can read this letter together. I wait for that day when you and I can be buddies and do those things together that we both will enjoy.

My love for you is far more than I could ever

express in words.

Give your mother a big hug and a kiss for me.
Until that wonderful day when we meet, love—
Daddy

Book II

June 10, 1949

Dear Harry:

I learned today that you are still alive. I don't know what to think. After all these years? I don't know you anymore—or you me. But I have never forgotten you.

When I heard the news that awful day about what had happened to you, I was devastated. I could not go on. Couldn't survive. Didn't want to. What else was there for me to live for?

The baby died so suddenly. God took him from me—I've always believed that and probably always will. He died in his sleep. But I can't think about that now. It still hurts too much, even after all these years.

You can't imagine what an effort it is for me to write this letter. Writing to you again—after I thought (We *all* thought!) you were dead. Am I dreaming? Can this be real? Are you actually…alive?

When Streete Wilder knocked on my door today, I knew instantly who he was. Not what you would think, that after seven years you couldn't *possibly* remember someone whom you barely even knew and hadn't thought about for so long. But it was like he had never left. And maybe in my mind he hadn't—maybe in some small area of my brain you and he *were* still there—still together, after so long. Still a part of my world. Oh, my

God, I *must* be crazy for still feeling as I do!

Captain Streete Wilder, the same handsome officer who was so kind after I lost the baby. The same man who delivered your sweet letter written to our son (how that broke my heart again to know you loved your child so much but would never see him). And the same dear friend who came by on that dreadful Monday morning, March 23, 1942 (I shall never forget the date as long as I live.), and brought me the tragic news that your bomber had been shot down by the Germans, and you were missing!

How I cried for you. How I begged Captain Wilder to tell me it wasn't true! How I prayed to God you would be found alive and safe! I never heard any more. No news. Captain Wilder assured me he would do everything in his power to try to find out something. Anything. But he never heard. And then he told me, right before he left and returned my box of letters, that I must accept the worst: you were officially presumed either lost or dead.

And when Streete Wilder was transferred from Hargis Field two months later to go overseas, all hope of ever hearing any news of you again died. And so I buried the two greatest things of my life: our precious son and my love for you.

I have kept all my letters to you these past seven years. How many times I have read them over and over until finally I just quit. I hid them away in an old chest in the spare bedroom down the hall in my parents' house and swore I would never go in that room again. Too many memories I have tried so hard, for so long, to forget.

And then, I believe it was about five years ago, I

got an anonymous letter in the mail from Gary, Indiana. It was Streete's letter to you about our little boy's birth. How I cherished that letter! But oh, how it hurt all over again. I assumed it was sent from your parents. I guess they never knew about us and our love, or our little boy. But they had to know you were still alive! Why didn't they let me know? Why didn't *you* let me know? Surely, that's not asking too much of you or them?

Captain Streete Wilder at my front door, after seven years, with news that you were still alive! A voice from the dead! Resurrected! I don't know how I handled it this afternoon when he came here and told me that. I don't know if I can accept this or even that I *want* to. All is different now. From this day forward, will I ever be the same again?

Streete walked into my new house like he belonged here. Like he had never left. When he sat down on the couch in my living room and lit a cigarette—time meant nothing. Only a brief passing of years. Memories never die. They sink like rocks thrown in a pond, but they're still there—still the same. Only hidden. Oh, to see him sitting there on my couch! I thought, at first, that he must be a ghost or maybe that I had lost my mind.

"I have some interesting news for you, Emily," he finally said. "Harry Devening is alive. I heard from him. A telephone call last week. I drove down here from Memphis to let you know."

I was utterly speechless. No feelings. No emotion. Nothing but shocked silence. Then I said something totally stupid, "It has been so long. Why now? Why after all these years, Streete?"

"I don't know. I don't know what to think,

myself."

We talked all afternoon. Streete told me you called him last Friday from Indiana. He told me that, after your bomber was struck by artillery fire, you managed to parachute down but were captured by the Germans and sent to a prison camp near Frankfurt. He told me how your left leg was shattered in three places and that a German doctor had to finally amputate it. He said you stayed in that dreadful prison camp, forgotten and presumed dead, until the War in Europe was over. When the Allies finally freed you, Streete said you went to some hospital in England for several months to convalesce and that you stayed in England for two years, trying to forget the War and all the atrocities you witnessed.

Streete told me that's when you started drinking. (I guess to forget all the pain and sorrow?) He told me you finally came back to the States and went from Army hospital to Army hospital, trying to get some help, until you eventually returned home to your parents in Indiana.

But still you kept on drinking until you almost killed yourself. Why? Then you finally got help. That was all Streete told me. Very matter of factly. No other details. I felt like Streete Wilder was telling me some sad story he had just read in *Life Magazine*!

And now you're ready to start living again. Just like that. No news from you or your parents in seven long years. Nothing but the letter from Streete to you that they must have found among your possessions after you were presumed dead. Did your parents know you were alive during those prison years in Germany? When you were in that Army hospital in England? Or were you so devastated from this tragedy that you didn't even contact them?

Why did you abandon us all, and what am I to think now? Am I supposed to believe you needed seven years to sort out your life? Have you been so destroyed that you couldn't let anyone know you were still alive? Perhaps your drinking was a convenient crutch? Was it really to forget the pain—or was it merely to hide behind?

And now you say you want to make amends and see me again? And you asked Streete Wilder to come here—after all this time—to apologize for you? To ask me if I can forgive you and will I see you again? Of all the *nerve*! What am I to think, Harry Devening? What the hell am I supposed to say?

Oh, Harry—why didn't you let me know you were still alive? I don't care about your leg! That makes you no less of a man to me. If I had known you were still alive, I would have joined you in England and gladly lived with you anywhere. Couldn't I have helped nurse you back to health? Surely this would have been better than almost drinking yourself to death! Just to forget?

But you haven't forgotten—have you, my love? Nor have I.

How will I sleep tonight after what I learned today? I fear that when I awake in the morning, this will be only a dream. Harry. My precious love. Please say it is true and that you really are alive and coming here again. Dear...sweet...Jesus.

Emily

June 11, 1949

Dear Harry:

Where do I begin to tell you everything that has transpired? How do I account for these seven long years that I thought you were dead?

When Streete returned to my house again this morning, I asked if he knew where I could contact you. Where I could send some letter to you. Call you. Anything! But he said you would contact me. Not to call. Why? And how long am I to wait?

I am a fool for wanting to see you again, I know that. But I have never stopped loving you.

I must tell you, though—I am not the same. Things change, people change, and we never tell each other.

Streete Wilder said today that the years had been good to me. How wonderful that was to hear, but how odd that sounded coming from him.

I fixed him lunch in my new home. I have become quite the independent woman since the War ended. One day I will explain why.

"Why have you come back here?" I asked him after we finished lunch and went into the living room. He lit a cigarette and took a long drag from it without answering. "Why didn't you just call me, Streete? You didn't have to ride all the way down from Memphis just to tell me. That must have taken you several hours."

"It's really an easy drive down here," he told me.

"And it was worth it," he said. "Trust me, it was worth every mile of it."

"How did you find me?"

"It wasn't hard, Emily. Hamilton isn't *that* big, you know, and everyone knows Miss Emily Hodge."

"Yes, don't remind me. It's one of the main things I hate about this town."

"So why don't you move to a big city like Memphis? Lots going on there. Plenty to do and see. When did you move into this house?" he asked, surveying the room. "Kinda small, but cozy."

"About two years ago, and it suits my needs. I'm very happy here. No old memories to haunt me here. I like new houses; they don't groan at night."

"I wouldn't know. I live in an old apartment in the middle of the city."

"You never answered my question, Captain Wilder. Why did you—"

"Please," he interrupted, "no one's called me 'Captain' in years. I was promoted to major before I was discharged, but please call me Streete."

"Congratulations. Now, why did you come back here? Why didn't you just call and let me know about Harry?"

"I don't know," he said, crossing his other knee and taking a sip of coffee. Then he took another drag on his cigarette before exhaling a huge smoke ring. "Maybe...maybe I wanted to see you again? See if you were still the same beautiful woman I used to know and care about."

"Tell me more about Harry, Major Wilder," I replied, somewhat uneasily.

"Can I ask you something, Emily? And I don't

mean to be personal, but why have you never married?"

"Why have *you* never married?" I quickly responded.

"Oh, I thought about it once. Almost did, right after the War. But I didn't love her; never would have. Do you think that's selfish, Emily?"

"I guess that depends on whether she loved you." Then, bringing the coffee cup to my lips to hide my nervousness, I asked him, "How did you meet her?"

"That doesn't matter now. What's done is done." Streete looked straight in my eyes and asked the strangest thing. "Why do you still love Harry, Emily? How could you possibly feel anything for that man after all these years?"

I set my cup and saucer down on the end table next to my chair, and then I said, "I never said I *do* still love Harry. I don't know what I feel, Streete."

"I think I do, but I don't understand. Emily, I hate to have to tell you this, but Harry Devening is not the same man you used to love."

"And I am not the same woman."

"No, you don't understand. The War changed him—drastically. His leg. Prison camp. Being a drunk all those years. In and out of hospitals…."

"I thought Harry was your friend, Major Wilder? Shouldn't you at least feel *some* sort of—"

"He is. Very much so. I just don't want to see you get hurt again. You've already suffered enough."

I got up and walked over to the front window and looked outside; my back was to Streete. Across Monmouth Avenue, in the front yard of a new house like mine, a little boy was throwing a baseball with his father. I thought, for just a second, how wonderful it would be if that were you and….

"Why do you care if I'm hurt again, Major Wilder? What difference could that possibly make to you?"

"I have to confess something, Emily," he said very slowly, almost apologetically.

I turned and faced him. He was looking down at the floor with his elbows resting on his knees, wringing his hands together when he said, "You remember that box of letters you asked me to deliver to Harry before he was shot down, before your baby boy died—the ones I returned to you before I was finally transferred overseas?"

"Yes; I still have them all. What about them?"

He paused for a moment; then he said, "Well, I know I shouldn't have, but I read them. Every one of them."

I swallowed a huge lump in my throat. "What? What did you just say? I don't believe this! How could you have done such an awful thing?"

"I know I shouldn't have. I had no right to invade your privacy like that. And you have every reason to hate me for—"

"Well, you did a damn fine job *resealing* them, I must admit! I'm sure this talent of yours came in quite handy during the War! Did you also read all my letters to Harry down at Camp Shelby?"

"That's not fair, Emily!" he said. "Yes, I did, but it wasn't the same thing. That was my job, as Commanding Officer, to screen all of my men's letters, to and from home."

"I can't believe this! I confided in you. You were supposed to be Harry's best friend. I entrusted you with something personal of mine to deliver to him—the man

I loved—and you betrayed both of us. You ought to be ashamed of yourself!"

Then he said, longingly, "I just had to see how you felt. It was so lonely out at that old airfield here. Nothing to do. No one to care about. No one to be with."

"What business was it of yours to know how I felt about Harry?"

"Because I knew how he felt about you, Emily! Don't you think he used to tell me at Camp Shelby while we were there? Hell, the two of us spent six months down there together!"

"What are you getting at? Why are you telling me all this now?"

"Wake up, Emily Hodge! Harry Devening doesn't love you—he never has and never will. Why do you think he never wrote you? Never called. Nothing. Don't be a damn fool! Hasn't he already hurt you enough?"

"Even if that's true, what concern is this of yours, Streete Wilder? You come back here after seven years and—"

"Because I love you, Emily! I fell in love with you the first time I ever laid eyes on you. And after I read all those beautiful letters of yours to a man who I knew didn't love you—never *would* love you—I had to come back here and tell you."

I was dumbfounded. I couldn't speak for several seconds. Then, I mumbled, "Streete, I don't, I don't know what to say. I had no idea you felt—"

"Don't say anything, Emily. There is nothing *to* say, not now. But I had to tell you how I felt. I don't expect a reply from you. Just give me a chance to show you."

"Show me—show me, how? You suddenly appear and tell me that you've been secretly in love with me for seven years, and now you want to 'show me'?"

"Yes, Emily, I do. All I ask is a chance. I know I can make up for all this lost time."

"This is crazy, you know. *I'm* crazy for even listening to this! I don't believe this is actually happening to me!"

"You can't say you don't feel *something* for me. I could see it in your eyes that day when I visited you in the hospital, right after—"

"You must leave now, Major Wilder," I abruptly told him. "You really must be going."

Then Streete came over to where I was standing. He placed both his hands on my upper arms and said, "Leave with me, Emily; come with me back to Memphis. We could have so much there together. There's no life for you in Hamilton. What will you do here—grow old, longing for some one-leg alcoholic who never loved you back?"

I slapped his face as hard as I could! I had never struck another human being before, but I hit him across his left cheek with all the anger I felt. "Get out of here! How dare you say that about Harry. How *dare* you!"

Then, as Streete was putting on his hat and opening the door to leave, he turned and said, "I'm sorry, Emily. I didn't mean to hurt you. I guess I'm the real fool for never telling you before how I felt."

I am so sorry, my love, for having to write you about this. Maybe some things are best left buried.

Emily

June 12, 1949

Dear Harry:

I am so ashamed over what happened yesterday when Streete Wilder came back to my house. I feel like my safe, secure world has been violated—taken advantage of. I cannot believe he said all those cruel things about you and that he could possibly have romantic feelings for me. How could he love a woman who has not been with another man for over eight years—who has not felt even a ripple of emotion for another human being since you left? I am terribly confused and upset by all this.

I am glad Streete has left and gone back to Memphis. I never want to see or hear from him again.

Love,
Emily

June 16, 1949

Dear Harry:

After our precious little boy died, I think I buried part of me with him in that tiny, white wicker casket. He was so sweet and beautiful. The dearest thing you could possibly imagine. When they brought him in to me after the delivery and I held him in my arms, how I cried that I had to give him away!

He looked so much like you. Thick, black hair. I saw his little eyes, and they were dark brown, just like yours. And he was such a big fellow. He seemed so healthy, so alert. Old Dr. Ernst told me that early the next morning he stopped breathing. His heart simply stopped, and he died in his sleep. No explanation; he just died. He never cried. Not once. Such a precious child. God took him away from me.

But I am so selfish to even think such a thing. For my sorrow, my loss, was nothing compared to what that couple from Jackson must have felt when they learned the baby they were going to adopt had died. I found out later that the couple asked to see our little boy before he was taken to the funeral home that day. I don't think Dr. Ernst permitted this, though. There really was no reason to. Funny, even though I never knew them—I felt so sorry for them. After all, it was their loss too.

After the death, Streete Wilder was such a good friend. And if it hadn't been for Wilma, I don't think I could have made it. She helped me through those awful months that followed. I can't tell you how many times I cried myself to sleep at night. Nothing helped. And it seemed the more I prayed, the worse I felt.

I have asked God many times over the past seven years to forgive me for what I did. I brought a sweet, innocent child into this world, and God punished him instead of me. Why He did not just take me instead, I shall never understand. God is so mysterious and aloof.

I will never forget the day I saw Captain Streete Wilder walking up the front steps of my parents' house, carrying my box of letters to you. I instantly knew something bad had happened. And when Streete told me the awful news that your bomber had been shot down, my world ended. Our baby's death, and the loss of you, were too much to bear. How I survived, I'm honestly not sure.

Life seemed so meaningless that winter and spring of 1942. Streete was transferred from Hargis Field to somewhere overseas, and I knew then it was hopeless to think I'd ever hear any more news about you. I became a recluse. I was mad at everyone and everything: the Germans, my parents, God—but especially myself. How I wanted to run away and die! I was so utterly alone and depressed that nothing really mattered anymore. Nothing at all.

Months passed and became years. But after the War finally ended, Hamilton seemed to change; so did I. I think I just woke up one day and decided I was tired of feeling sorry for myself and ready to rejoin the world.

There was a new enthusiasm in the air. It was the fall of 1945. Wilma had just started her last year of school at Tougaloo College. She got a full scholarship to go there. I believe I have written you before how smart Wilma is, and Tougaloo is a splendid learning institution for Negroes. I was so proud of her. She graduated in the top of her class, and then she got accepted to a teaching college in Pennsylvania that Dr. Aaron Geisenberger had helped her get into.

Mrs. Geisenberger passed away a year ago, but she was always so good to Wilma and took such a special interest in her. Wilma told me Mrs. Geisenberger used to send her money every month while she was at Tougaloo. I believe Mrs. Geisenberger left Wilma some more money when she died last year, because Wilma went out and bought herself a 1943 green Chevrolet, shortly after she moved back here to start teaching.

Will Bacon made the comment one day when he saw Wilma driving it down Cowan Street, where he lives now with his new wife, that it was the "tackiest" car he had ever seen.

Will moved back to Hamilton shortly after the War. We didn't communicate much at first. I was still quite the martyr, spending most of my time alone in my old upstairs bedroom in my parents' house. I don't remember if I was just afraid to move out on my own and start a life or if I truly felt some obligation to help my parents around the house. Probably a little of both.

Father had a stroke in November of 1944, so he had to retire as an alderman. And since he couldn't work anymore, he sold the furniture store shortly thereafter to this young couple who moved up here from Baton Rouge. I felt like Mother needed me around the house to help her and to look after Father. Thinking back, though, I probably used that as an excuse to stay home and hide from the world.

I think now one of the best things that happened to me, and I'm sure it was Divine Providence, was Father's buying this new house for me on Monmouth Avenue. (It's away from downtown in a new area near Dillon Park.) It's a small, yellow-shingle, two-bedroom bungalow. Very modest, but I have modern furniture and a new stove and refrigerator. I'm very happy here and content. I feel sure I will be here the rest of my days, as it really is all I need.

When I'm not with Wilma, I spend most of my time reading and working in my garden; both these activities give me great pleasure. I have often considered attending Hamilton Junior College at night and working toward some degree, as this would greatly please my mother. She never says so, but I can tell she believes I am doing nothing with my life.

I thought I would never hear from Will Bacon again. His momma finally had to be committed to the State Mental Hospital in Jackson to keep from drinking herself to death. That pathetic woman got drunk one night at the Confederate Ball and took off all her clothes. Mother swore Mrs. Bacon had started drinking Red Crow whiskey at lunch that day with some of her friends and never quit. When she went to the party that evening, she supposedly told someone that modern women look utterly ridiculous in hoop skirts, so she took off everything in the bathroom but her bra and panties and walked out smoking a cigarette. I'm sure Mrs. Bacon was quite a sight, and Mother swears several older ladies swooned when they saw her. The next day, Sheriff Creel took Mrs. Bacon up to the Hospital in his patrol car.

Poor Will. I would never have moved back here if I were him, and I'm frankly surprised he did. Besides the fact that I was still spending most of my time at home helping Mother take care of Father, shortly after Will moved back he began courting this notorious older woman, so I wouldn't have seen him much, anyway.

Will and Madeleine Pou were the talk of the town! You would think after that horrifying scene his momma caused at the Confederate Ball, Will would have been too embarrassed to ever show his face in Hamilton again. And then for him to take up with a harlot like Madeleine Pou—well, I was simply appalled!

I flatly told him so when I bumped into him alone one day downtown. But Will Bacon has always had the sensitivity of a mule, and I don't believe anything ever fazes him. "I think you're just jealous, Emily. You're jealous because I'm dating someone who has more money than you," Will said.

"That is totally preposterous," I quickly told him. "I couldn't care *less* how much money Madeleine Pou has. Besides, she'd be flat broke if her last husband hadn't died young."

"Fortunately for me," Will quipped, "Stanley Pou also died rich. Good day, Miss Hodge, I must be going now. Madeleine needs me to bring her something."

Will then marched off around the corner, and I never got a chance to tell him what I really thought. He sure has his nerve! The very idea—his telling me I was jealous of her money. That tramp?

When Will and Madeleine Pou later got married, I thought I would die. Madeleine is old enough to be his older sister! She must be at least thirty-five, and Will is only twenty-five—ten years' difference. Simply outrageous! So I absolutely refused to go to their wedding. I heard no one went. Served the little fool right.

Will never told me much about his stint in the Navy, and I would never have dared to ask. I'm sure he would have claimed he rose to "Rear Admiral" and was decorated twice for sinking Japanese ships. After he moved back here, he seemed to flounder for a while, living all alone in his momma's house behind the hotel.

Then he met Madeleine Pou at our American Legion Christmas Eve party at the hotel and started (so I heard) an "impetuous romance." I hate to believe Will Bacon married Madeleine Pou for her money, but I feel sure this is the case. Madeleine even put him to work in Stanley Pou's printing shop, which Will is now running. Frankly, though, it's the best thing that could have happened to Will, as I doubt he could have gotten any other job here in town.

Wilma said, "Now Will Bacon is set for life—a rich, older wife to take the place of his momma. He must be in hog heaven!"

I can't imagine that he's happy, though.

Love,

Emily

June 20, 1949

Dear Harry:

There was much talk in town today about the brutal murder of a young colored man who lived on Steam Plant Road. Things are happening here that I just don't understand.

His name was Walter Malone, and they found him last night hung from a tree near his house with a note stuck to the bottom of his trousers that read, "This damn n—— tried to steal our job!"

The newspaper reported that Walter's wife and three small children watched in horror as "several men in white hooded sheets drug him from his house and brutally beat him with sticks. Then they tied a rope around his feet and drug him from the back of one of their pickup trucks down the dirt road in front of his house." They found Walter about two miles down the road, lynched from an old pecan tree. The sheriff also found a huge burning cross in the field across the road.

What kind of evil *monsters* would do such a horrible thing as this?

There is a meeting Saturday night after his service out at Cemetery Hill Baptist Church where Wilma attends. She and I are planning to go. Father has advised strongly against my attending a Negro political meeting out in the country at night, but I must support Wilma in her efforts to fight this terrible injustice.

I care more about doing what is right than I do about what other people might think.

Love,

Emily

P.S. Do not worry about me, Harry. I am not the naïve young lady you used to know.

June 22, 1949

Dear Harry:

Wilma came by today after school and we talked about Walter Malone. I'm happy she got the new teaching job she applied for. I never thought her first teaching assignment at the colored elementary school in the county was challenging enough for her. She seemed so frustrated trying to teach fourth and fifth grade colored children how to read and write, and it was such a long drive from her momma's house. The new colored high school in town, where Wilma will teach this fall, is much more to her liking and abilities.

"They murdered that young man, Emily; you know that, don't you?" Wilma asked me as we drank coffee in the kitchen. "They killed him simply because he was trying to get a job at the new tool plant. They dragged Walter screaming and hollering from his house in front of his wife and kids and beat him with sticks like he was a damn snake. Then they dragged him down a dirt road and lynched him—just because he was trying to find work to support his family. That isn't right, Emily; it just isn't right."

"I met Walter's wife once, Wilma. I didn't know Walter, but I met his wife about four months ago. Mother and I drove Father out to Steam Plant Road one Sunday afternoon to buy some mustard greens from an old farmer he knows, and I met Sarah. She was there buying some—"

"We've got to do something, Emily. Sarah's all alone now, with three children to support. How's she going to take care of them now, without Walter?"

"I'm sure we can probably raise a fund for her, Wilma. I'll be happy to ask Father for a donation, and I'm sure Madeleine Bacon will help. Will swears that Madeleine has a tender heart inside that tough exterior of hers."

"A few handouts from some rich white folks aren't going to bring Walter back." Wilma lit a Kool cigarette; then she added, "Momma said Walter probably would have gotten that die cutter job at the tool plant."

"Walter was as good as any of those white men who applied for the job, I'm sure."

"Except he was colored. That was his only mistake, and it cost him his life."

"What do you think will come of this?"

"Hell, Emily—*nothing* will come of this! You know as well as I do that nobody in this town is gonna do one damn thing about it!"

"Father said Sheriff Creel knows who some of the men are who killed Walter."

"Damn right he knows! He knows who *all* of them are! 'Klanners'—every damn one of 'em! You think he's going to do anything about it, though? If Sheriff Creel even tried to arrest one of those redneck farm boys, they'd string him up quick as they did Walter Malone! Emily, nothing's going to happen—nothing at all. Just another colored person who got lynched in Mississippi for trying to live like a white person."

"Surely there's *something* we can do?" I asked her.

Wilma seemed to be talking to herself when she

said, as if I weren't there anymore, "It's really *our* fault, though. We as a people, I mean. We have no voice, no rights. Nothing. No one rises up for us or ever speaks out for us. Our preachers have the power to influence us—tell us what to do. But they're afraid to. Too scared they might offend God, maybe? I don't know. Maybe they think it's God's will or something that we stay oppressed forever? I can't accept that. It ain't natural to be that way. Never has been; never will be."

"What do you think will happen at your church meeting on Saturday night, Wilma?"

"What difference does it make to you what happened to Walter Malone or to any colored person, for that matter? You're not one of us. How could you possibly understand how we feel or what we've endured all these years? Wouldn't it be easier just to pray to your white God for us and forget it?"

"How can you sit in my house and say that, Wilma? I *do* care—you *know* I care! You're my best friend, and I want to help. You're right, I don't understand how it feels to be colored, but I do want to see the criminals who murdered Walter Malone brought to justice."

"Justice, Emily? There'll never be any justice for my people here. Long as we sit by, don't rise up and stand for what's right, there'll never be any justice for any of us!"

I couldn't help believing Wilma was probably right. When she finally left in her green Chevrolet, it was already dark. I noticed that a light on in the new house across the street was quickly turned off as soon as she left, and I could tell someone in there was watching her through their Venetian blinds as she drove away into the night.

That evening, I prayed for Sarah Malone and that God would speak to Wilma and let her know that He cares for colored people too.

Love,

Emily

P.S. I wish I had told Wilma before she left that "some of the best gifts from God come in boxes wrapped with ribbons of sorrow." I must remember to tell her that the next time I see her. I know that quote will make her feel better; it has always helped me.

June 24, 1949

Dear Harry:

"Absolutely, positively not!" is what Mother yelled over the telephone at me when I told her this morning I was going to a "political meeting" at a colored church on Saturday night. "Have you totally lost your mind, Emily Edna Hodge?" she asked me. "You have no idea what they do in those colored churches at night. I simply will not have my daughter going to a Negro Protestant church—and that's final!"

"Mother," I said, "I'm only going to support Wilma. She wants to organize a group to protest the Walter Malone hanging."

"What business is that of yours? Why should you get involved in their affairs? And that Wilma Watson friend of yours is nothing but a troublemaker—always has been. I simply hate that you still run with her."

"Mother, Wilma and I are like sisters."

"Listen to me, Emily—and for once you had best heed what I'm saying. No respectable white girl this day and time has any business fooling with a bunch of Negroes! No good can come from it—don't you understand that?"

"All I understand, Mother," I said, trying to soften the conversation, "is that Wilma is my best friend and she needs my help and support right now. Why is this so difficult for you to grasp?"

"How can you possibly help those people, Emily? They won't even help themselves! Let Wilma help them—she's nothing but a 'rabble-rouser,' anyway."

"What do you mean by that?"

"You know exactly what I mean. Half the town knows what I mean. You think we don't know what she preached to those colored students last year? You think we don't know what she used to tell them? 'Graduate from high school. Go to college and get a degree. Don't dig ditches and cut grass all your life like your daddies. Rise up and speak out for your rights…' *Rights*—my God, Emily! What does a Negro know about rights? For that matter, what does a Negro know about *anything*?"

"How dare you say such a cruel thing, Mother! I'm ashamed of you! And what about Walter Malone's rights? Didn't he have the right to live his life? To raise his children and support a family? To watch his children grow up? Didn't he have a right to apply for a good job and not be lynched by the damn Klan because of it?"

There was a deafening silence on the other end of the phone line for a few seconds. Then Mother finally said, slowly, "Emily, you don't know what you're about to get involved in. Listen to me, dear. We both know you've made some serious mistakes with those people in the past, but is that any reason to throw away the rest of your life—for people like them?"

"I'm not throwing away my life, Mother. I'm finally starting to *live* it!"

"Yes…you…are! Because once you set foot in that colored church, you're no better than one of them. Once you side with those Negroes, there's no turning back. No decent white family in Hamilton will *ever* accept you into their home again."

"Does that include you, Mother?"

"At this point, I'm not sure," she simply said. Then she hung up the phone.

Harry, oh dear Harry! How has my life turned out like this? When we first met, eight years ago, I never dreamed I would one day be so rejected and alone. Am I relegated now to spend the rest of my days yearning for our lost love in a town where I'm not received by anyone but colored people? Am I to grow old knowing that even my parents have shunned me?

Where have I gone wrong? How did I become like this? Has God cursed me forever for giving myself to you before marriage? Is He still punishing me for that terrible sin I committed eight years ago? Will He never forgive me? Oh, dear God, how I regret what I did, and how I wish I could change the past!

When will you return, my love? When will you come back here and rescue me from all this hatred and bigotry? Will I ever see your precious face again? Am I still dreaming that Streete Wilder actually said you were coming back? I must call Streete today and find out where you are! I cannot stand this loneliness any longer. I feel like I am going to die; perhaps I should.

Do you understand how I feel, my love? Am I crazy to feel as I do—still loving you and wanting to do something about the horrible injustice in this town that has hurt you, me, Will Bacon, and now poor Walter Malone? How I long to know what you think.

Emily

Next was this telegram from Memphis, Tennessee, also dated June 24, 1949:

MISS EMILY HODGE
110 MONMOUTH AVENUE
HAMILTON, MISSISSIPPI
REGRET I MISSED YOUR CALL THIS MORNING STOP AM LEAVING BY TRAIN TODAY FOR NEW ORLEANS STOP WILL CATCH BUS TO HAMILTON NEXT THURSDAY STOP MUST SEE YOU AGAIN STOP HAVE IMPORTANT NEWS STOP
LOVE
STREETE WILDER
ASSISTANT VICE-PRESIDENT
COMMERCE BANK OF MEMPHIS

June 25, 1949

Dear Harry:

I had the strangest visit from Stephen and Genevieve Brandon today. They dropped by after lunch, unannounced, and I'm afraid my little house really was a sight. In her usual way, Genny made a cursory excuse about why they didn't call first (something about their not wanting me to go to any trouble), but I was quite embarrassed for not having cleaned up. Genny seemed amazed that any human being could live in such a small home, but I assured her I was very comfortable here and that a two-bedroom bungalow was absolutely perfect for me.

"Did your father furnish this place for you?" Genny inquired, carefully inspecting every piece of furniture in the house.

"Yes. Just before he sold his store."

"But it's all so, so *modern*?" she said. "I thought you preferred antiques, Emily? I simply couldn't stand to live in a house without nice antiques."

"I prefer them, Genny, when I can afford them. Until I start working, I'm grateful for what I have."

Then she walked down the hall. "I like the way they built this cut-out area in the wall for a telephone. That's so…convenient."

"Yes," I replied. "I spend a lot of time in this hall talking on the phone, but the standing gets old."

Then she went into my bedroom and looked around like a child at a county fair. "Who are all these pictures of, Emily? I don't believe I know any of these people. Are they from Hamilton?"

"No. Those were just some friends of—"

"Isn't this Harry Devening?" she asked, picking up the large silver frame on my dresser.

"Yes."

"My, wasn't he dapper standing next to that nice airplane. What ever became of him, Emily? Did he finally move back north to Indiana or wherever he was from?" Then she picked up the smaller frame next to it. "And this is a lovely photo of you. What beach was this made at—Biloxi?"

"Yes."

She went and sat down on my bed. Thank God I had made it that morning—Genny would have spread it all over town that I never made my bed.

"You know, I always loved this mahogany bed of yours. Wasn't it your grandmother's? Remember how we used to jump on it when we were little girls, and your mother would get so mad at us?"

"Yes. I do. And my mother still gets mad at me."

"What?" she asked, turning around to face me.

"Nothing. So, Genny, why don't we rejoin Stephen in the den, and I'll make us some coffee. Would you care for some lemon pound cake? I just made it yesterday."

"No. Coffee would be perfect. Thank you, Emily."

As I walked out of my bedroom, I could tell that Genevieve was staring again at your framed picture. It made me uneasy that she was looking at you like that, and I sensed her reason for visiting was something other than just to be social.

We sat down and drank coffee, and then Stephen said, "I'm glad we have this chance to visit, Emily. How are you doing?"

"I'm just fine, Stephen. How is your law practice coming along? I understand you're the managing partner in your firm now?"

"Oh, yes," Genny interrupted before Stephen could answer, "and we're all very proud of him! Stephen loves the practice of law and works so hard at it."

"Don't let Genny fool you, Emily. There's really nothing glamorous about practicing law. And when they make you a partner, it only means you have to start helping to pay for the utilities and the secretaries."

"You're way too modest, Stephen," I told him. "Everyone in town knows you're an excellent attorney."

"He'll be a judge one day—I'm sure of that," Genevieve offered, seeing her husband was blushing and somewhat embarrassed.

I decided to change the subject. "I'm really glad you both came by this morning. Glad you're finally seeing my new house. Sorry it's so messy, though."

"No, Emily, it's fine. It's a very nice home," Stephen offered. "And just the right size for you."

"Who built this little house, Emily," Genny asked, "that Italian fellow? What was his name again?"

"Sonopoli. Vincent Sonopoli."

"Where was he from? Did he fight for us or Italy during the War?

"I don't know, Genny. I didn't think it mattered to ask him when he was building my new house."

"Emily," Stephen said, and I could tell from the

"lawyer" tone of his voice and the way he firmly placed the cup and saucer down on the coffee table in front of them that he was ready to start talking business, "Genevieve and I have come to discuss a personal matter with you."

I paused for a moment before I said, "It sounds serious, Stephen."

"It is—very serious. Your mother telephoned me yesterday and asked if I would visit you concerning the political meeting tonight in that colored church out at Cemetery Hill."

I said nothing at first. I really wasn't surprised this was why Stephen and Genevieve had come to see me, but I didn't know exactly what to say. I was embarrassed that my mother had called him and mad, at the same time, that she was still trying to interfere in my life. "Stephen, I don't really think my going to a colored church tonight is all that serious."

"Emily Hodge—are you kidding me?" Genny demanded to know, slapping both hands on her knees. "Do you have any idea what could happen to you in a Negro church? My Lord, Emily—I've heard it all, or so I thought—but I can't believe you're serious. No self-respecting white person from Hamilton would ever…even…consider…."

"Genny, you sound just like my mother."

"As well I should! At least I don't sound like some 'Negro-lover'!"

"Emily," Stephen interrupted, leaning forward to make his point, "I don't care about your feelings toward Negroes; I really don't. What concerns me, though, are the feelings of a whole lot of white people in this town toward them."

"Yes, Stephen," I said, "that concerns me too. That is precisely why I plan to go tonight with Wilma Watson to that meeting at her church. Someone from the white community has to let them know that—"

"Oh, really, Emily—don't tell me you're hanging out with *her* again? She's no good, Emily—or didn't you know she stole money from that old Jewish woman?"

"Mrs. Geisenberger?"

"Yes. That was her."

"That's an outright lie, Genevieve Brandon! Eva Geisenberger *loved* Wilma—treated her like a daughter!"

"Says you. I say that Negro stole the money to buy that old Chevrolet she drives around in like she was white. She's just asking for trouble, Emily. Listen, I'm one of your oldest and dearest friends, and I'm only trying to warn you—don't you understand?"

"Warn me?" I asked. "Warn me from what, pray tell? Just what are you trying to say, Genny?"

"I think what Genny is trying to say, Emily," Stephen interjected, "is that it might be a good idea if you don't get involved in this matter tonight."

I looked Stephen straight in his gray eyes and said, "Then who *will* get involved, Stephen? You? Your prestigious law firm?" And I said to Genny, "Or maybe your garden club friends will take up a collection for Sarah Malone and her three children, Genevieve?"

"For those uppity Negroes? Not hardly. Don't be a fool, Emily. That Walter Malone Negro got *exactly* what he deserved."

When Genevieve Brandon said this, I knew at that moment my life would never be the same. Something ripped through me like an explosion. The reality of what she had just said was like shrapnel hitting me. I felt like I was floating on the ceiling of my tiny den, listening to some hunter brag how he had just killed a deer. I listened in disbelief—shock—to Genevieve expound on how it was time for the white people of Mississippi to "teach these modern Negroes a lesson and put them back in their rightful place." She spoke of Walter Malone—not as if he were human but as if he were nothing more than an example that the rest of his "kind" should heed.

When they finally left, I didn't even follow them to the door or say goodbye. The last words I remember hearing was Genny's admonition to "think about what we've said, Emily, for your own sake." And I did think about it. Every word she said. All afternoon.

I thought about Sarah Malone, her three helpless children, and wondered how they would survive. I thought about Walter Malone and how terrified he must have been when six drunk men in white hooded sheets pulled him from his bed at two o'clock in the morning and beat him with sticks in front of his family. I thought about how Walter had been dragged by a pickup truck and then strung from a tree like a dead deer for nothing more than applying for a decent job. And then I thought about you, Harry, and how you understood this kind of hatred and bigotry.

I also thought about how different Genevieve Brandon and I now were. Sadly, we had grown so far apart. I wondered how two people from the same small town in Mississippi, from the same background, and who once had been so close, could now be so different.

Whatever it is that has led me to this extreme point

in my life *must* be from God. And though I do not understand it and probably never will, and though I am frightened by what Genevieve said today, I am convinced in my heart that I am right. How could I feel otherwise?

I miss you terribly,
Emily

This newspaper article was folded inside a plain, blue envelope, unsealed. It was dated Sunday, June 26, 1949.

Hamilton, Mississippi. Violence broke out last night at the Cemetery Hill Baptist Church north of Hamilton, where about fifty Negro adults and children were meeting over the recent death of Walter Malone, a local Negro from the Steam Plant Road community. Malone was found last Sunday hanging from a pecan tree about two miles east of his house. Suicide is suspected.

According to reports from the sheriff's office, the Negroes were illegally gathered and planned to organize a demonstration in protest for their "civil rights." Violence erupted when local white citizens, who had peacefully gathered outside the church, began chanting at the colored people inside. When several colored men rushed outside to confront the crowd, a fight broke out, and the white citizens defended themselves with rocks and sticks. Several Negro men and women were hurt and had to be taken in trucks to the General Hospital.

The Sheriff's Patrol was quick to respond to the scene. They called this an "unfortunate incident" and ordered the rest of the Negroes to go home. Rev. Ernest Washington, the colored church's preacher, and Wilma Watson, a local Negro teacher who helped organize the protest, were arrested for illegal gathering and inciting a riot. No other arrests were made.

28 June 1949
14 Ranier Street
Gary, Indiana

My Dear Emily—

Can you forgive me for not contacting you these past eight years? How often I have thought of you and the time we had together, but how afraid I have been to see you again.

Why? I don't know. I realize now you were the best thing that ever came into my life—you and our little boy. How I just wanted to see him. When I heard from Streete, before I was shot down and captured, that our little boy had died and that you were engaged to marry someone else, I was devastated.

I prayed to die in that prisoner camp in Frankfurt. I cannot describe the atrocities I witnessed every day. And knowing I would never see our little boy and maybe never see you again—there was no reason to hang on to life.

I knew my left leg would never heal. The pain was so unbearable that I finally begged this German doctor, who spoke perfect English, to cut it off. He was a kind man and seemed genuinely concerned—so unlike all the German guards there. I often confided to him about you and the little boy we lost. There can be humanity, even in the midst of Hell.

I don't intend to upset your life after all these

years; I merely want to see you again. Streete told me when I called him that you are no longer married. Though I don't feel like much of a man anymore, with only one leg, my feelings for you are unchanged.

I have enclosed a bus ticket for you to Gary, Indiana that you can use when you want. Please write to the address above and let me know when I may expect you.

My love,

Harry Devening, Jr.

P.S. I know you understand why I cannot come back there ever again.

July 3, 1949

Dear Harry:

I don't know that I will ever mail this letter to you, for I can't believe what I'm about to say. I'm not even sure what to think, much less what to do about your letter of June 28, but please let me try to explain.

More than anything else in the world, I want to see you again. Our years apart mean nothing to me, for you have never left my heart. And you must not think yourself any less of a man, for I will always regard you as the bravest man I have ever known.

There is so much I want to say to you. I have written several letters to you since I learned from Streete Wilder that you were still alive—now they all seem so pointless that I will maybe destroy them. How foolish and selfish I have been to not realize what you have been through.

I have never married or ever known another man since you. Streete Wilder, who I always thought was your friend, lied to you. I can only assume he was jealous of our love when he told you I was engaged to marry another man. I have never loved anyone but you, and I never will.

Streete arrived here by bus three days ago from New Orleans. When he came here last month and told me you were still alive, it was like a message from God—a miracle! An answer to my most ardent prayer!

But then he said I was a fool for still loving you after all these years. He claimed *he* was in love with me. Now he has come here again and asked me a second time to come back with him to Memphis to be his wife—after what he did?! I have no feelings for Streete Wilder but utter contempt for betraying you and lying about me. I told him in no uncertain terms to never contact me again. I could never love a man like him! He has called me twice already today, but I have no intention of ever speaking to him again.

So much has happened here lately that I don't know when I could possibly leave for Indiana. Yes, I want to see you—more than you could possibly know. But my dear friend, Wilma, is in trouble and desperately needs my help now.

Wilma is deeply involved in the murder protest of Walter Malone. I have never seen so much hatred in this town. Ever since the tire plant closed two years ago, people have been desperate for jobs. There are so many men here, colored and white, who came back after the War and are still looking for work. It is sad to see them all hanging around the courthouse downtown—they just sit there on benches all day with nothing to do but smoke cigarettes and tell War stories.

When the new tool factory opened six months ago and began hiring, there must have been two hundred men who waited in line for ten hours to apply for the sixty jobs. The sheriff's deputies had to be called to keep order after several fights broke out between men shoving each other out of line. No Negroes would have dared to go by that day to apply for a job.

But Walter Malone didn't think the color of his skin should matter. So he later applied for a die cutter position at the factory, and it cost him his life.

Oh, Harry, it was awful what those white men did to Walter! Wilma and Reverend Washington organized a meeting to raise some money for Walter's wife and three children. I went with Wilma because the Negroes here have to know that some white people in Hamilton *do* care.

I was proud of Wilma when she got up in front of the congregation to speak. She spoke so passionately about her people and how much they have suffered. She reminded them of the countless struggles and hardships they have endured and how Jesus has always seen them through. She told them that no Negro should be afraid to apply for a decent job, and that Walter Malone will have died in vain if colored folks don't rise up for their rights.

We all knew there might be trouble. Wilma informed me on the way to the church that she had recently received an anonymous letter in the mail that had threatened her life for being a "damn n—— trouble-maker." I was so scared when she told me this and even suggested to Wilma that we not attend the meeting.

But Wilma reminded me, "If we don't do it now, Emily—who will? If we don't help these people now—who will? We can't just do nothing, Emily, because we're afraid. 'Cause if we don't—we're just as guilty as those damn Klanners who murdered Walter."

I knew in my soul Wilma was right, and I felt like a coward for being so afraid. Then I remembered how brave you were and the sacrifice you made, Harry, for what you believed in.

We were all standing, holding hands and singing,

"Nobody knows the trouble I've seen; nobody knows but Jesus," when the first rock came crashing through the left front window near the pulpit. Several trucks had driven up while Reverend Washington was passing a collection hat around for Sarah Malone, but I had already seen approaching headlights through a window before they got there, about a half mile down the road.

Wilma and I held each other's hand so tightly when we saw them, but Reverend Washington said not to fear because God was in control.

Then those men got out of their trucks and started hollering (you could tell they were all drunk), "What you n——s doin' in there? You n——s better get on home! You n——s ain't stealin' no more jobs!" And that's when one of them tossed a rock through the window that almost hit Reverend Washington's wife, Mildred. Several colored men inside the church ran outside and confronted the white men, and then a big fight broke out.

Even from inside the church I could hear people being hit over the head with sticks and clubs. There was so much confusion; it was so dark, and everything happened so fast—like a nightmare. And then I saw red lights flashing down the road, headed our way. The patrol cars were there so quickly that they must have known what was going to happen, but they did nothing to prevent it. "This is so wrong!" I ran outside with Wilma and yelled at them. "This is all so wrong!"

There were eight or nine colored men and women lying on the ground, bleeding and crying. Most of the windows in our cars and trucks had been shattered with clubs and rocks, and every window in Wilma's Chevrolet had been broken. When Wilma saw what had happened to her car, she started to run over and jump on this white teenage boy who was standing next to it with a baseball bat in his hand. I held her back because I knew what he would have done to her if she had run over to him. None of those white men dared come inside, though. No doubt they were all "God-fearing Christians."

After the sheriff's deputies finally broke up the fight, we all went outside to help those who were hurt. Old Mr. Ike, Wilma's great-uncle, was sitting up against a cedar tree next to the steps out front with his skull cracked open, bleeding down his shirt.

He was the first one we put in the back of one of the pickups. I helped load the rest of the injured, and some of the men and women drove them back into town to the hospital. Then the fifteen or so white men who were there left in their pickup trucks, laughing and drinking beer like nothing had happened. Sheriff Creel and his three deputies ordered the rest of the colored people to go home, but they arrested Wilma and Reverend Washington and took them to jail. Driving back into Hamilton alone that night in Wilma's car, with glass all over the seats and floorboards, I have never been so angry and ashamed in my life.

Wilma and Reverend Washington were released from the county jail late Monday morning, and I met her there to take her home.

"Damn those Klanners," Wilma said when we walked down the front steps of the courthouse and she saw her car. "They ruined it! They destroyed my beautiful green car! It'll never look the same again!"

"The windows can be replaced, Wilma," I tried to assure her.

"I know who they were, Emily," Wilma said as we got inside her car. "I recognized two of those white men out there Saturday night who did this. I didn't see either one of them at first, but I recognized them soon as I caught a glimpse of their faces in a headlight. You remember that old redneck, Harlan Scruggs, and his son, Eddie, who attacked Will Bacon before the War?"

"Are you sure Eddie Scruggs was there last night, Wilma? It was so dark. I really couldn't tell—"

"I'm positive it was him. I used to see Eddie Scruggs hanging around downtown two, three times a week on my way home from school. Lots of times he and his Army buddies would hoot at me and holler something nasty when I drove by. I usually didn't pay them any mind—but I'm sure that was him with that younger cousin of his, Nolan, the one who survived the War, last night. I couldn't recognize anyone else, it was so dark and all. But I spotted those two in the light.

"And Reverend Washington said in the cell this morning he heard it was Eddie and Nolan Scruggs and four of their friends who beat and killed Walter. He didn't know about old man Harlan, though. Reverend Washington thinks he probably put 'em all up to it. They're all a bunch of Klanners—whole lot of them. Uncle Ike swore all those farm boys joined the Klan soon as they got laid off from the tire plant. Blamed the 'n——s' for losing their jobs! Can you believe that, Emily? Can you? No different than that damn Hitler, blaming the Jews for—"

"So what should we do about this?" I asked Wilma as she started her car and we drove away.

"I already told the sheriff about it, Emily. Reverend Washington begged me not to say 'nothing 'bout nothing.' Said it was dangerous to be telling on white folks around here. 'Hell,' I said, 'I've been talking about white folks in Hamilton all my life—I'm not scared of them!' So I told Sheriff Creel everything I knew about Eddie and Nolan Scruggs and their damn friends. Then he let us go; simple as that."

On the way back to my house, Wilma told me about the dream she had again last night. She calls it her "special dream" because she knows it comes from Jesus.

"I've had this dream before," she said, "several times since I was a little girl. Usually, after I went to bed real tired or was praying hard to Jesus before I fell asleep. Momma used to claim the 'Spirit' crept into my room at night and 'touched' me—that's how come I'd have the dream. I never believed that, though—about spirits. I just figured the Good Lord was trying to tell me something. Sometimes He's awful hard to figure out, though.

"In my dream, I'm always a little girl—about eleven or twelve—and I'm running through this huge field of green clover. It must be April or May, 'cause the sun's so warm on my face, and I can feel a south wind blowing through my hair. And I'm wearing the prettiest white poplin dress, that's flapping in the wind as I run along, and the thick clover feels so cool and fresh on my bare feet.

"Then I see this place up ahead. It's a circle about ten feet wide that's been fresh mowed or something. And I stop and just stare at it for a minute or so, but I always know that circle was cut there out of the clover 'specially for me, and I'm supposed to walk into the middle of that circle because it's a special place. So I do. And when I step into the middle of that circle and stand there a few seconds, *I* become special! And I start feeling like Jesus is smiling down real big at me. Then I see myself turn back around real…slowly, and when I see my face again, I'm not a little girl anymore but a grown woman, like now. And I'm raising my hands up to Heaven—palms first—and that's when it happens.

"Emily, it's the strangest thing. When I'm standing in that circle—that rising place—and I raise my palms up to Jesus, all these hundreds of beautiful balloons—every color you can imagine—start rising up out of the clover—from nowhere! It's like I'm the only one in the world who can make those beautiful balloons rise up to Heaven, and only when I'm standing in that rising place. And the higher and higher they go, the bigger and more colorful they get. And I'm just standing there holding my arms up with all these shiny balloons floatin' up all around me. Then I'm watching all this happen from a distance until the scene gets farther and farther away. That's when I wake up.

"I know it means something, Emily; I'm sure it does! What you think it means?"

"I don't know, Wilma; I'm not smart enough to understand dreams. I guess God will let you know that when He's ready."

Wilma pulled into my driveway, and I kissed her cheek and held her tiny brown hand for a few seconds before telling her goodbye and not to worry. As she drove away down the road, I felt like such a liar because I was so worried about her safety.

I hope you understand now why I cannot leave Wilma and come up to Indiana, for she greatly needs my support and friendship at this time.

I am going to see Will Bacon later this week and ask him to help me pay to have Wilma's car windows replaced. I feel sure he and Madeleine will help, as Wilma and Geneva have no money for this. I wouldn't dare ask Mother for a dime, though.

I want to see you again—more than anything else in the world, but I simply cannot leave Wilma now. I pray this whole matter will soon blow over and that life in Hamilton will return to normal. Still, knowing I must wait before I can see you again seems like an eternity.

Until that wonderful day—

All my love,

Emily

July 7, 1949

Dear Harry:

I was so wrong to have ever been critical of Madeleine Bacon, Will's wife. She is probably the most intriguing person I have ever met, and I regret not getting to know her sooner. Today was really the first time I have ever been around her, or she around me, and we both apologized to each other for being so distant.

As I told you, I refused to go to Will and Madeleine's wedding. How I regret that now. I was so upset with Will, then. You probably recall how Will Bacon has a special ability to offend people, and one day he said something to me when I bumped into him downtown that made me so angry—well, I simply refused to watch him get married. Mother and Father also did not attend but did send an appropriate gift. Mother asked if I wanted her to put my name on the reply card along with theirs, but I said no. Hardly anyone I know went to their wedding, and I heard later that only the usual Hamilton party-goers attended the gaudy reception at the Country Club. I was not embarrassed for Will, nor did I care.

Frankly, I thought, it served him right since everyone in town knew he only married Madeleine Pou for her deceased husband's money. And for Will Bacon to marry an older woman who had been with practically

every single man in town—well, it was simply
disgraceful.

I also was still feeling sorry for myself and
abandoned. Wilma hadn't graduated yet from teacher's
college, and I had recently moved out into my own
house—so I wasn't doing much socially, anyway. What
a fool I was and how ashamed I now feel for not
supporting Will's decision to marry Madeleine and for
not giving her a chance. Sometimes I fear I am no
different than all the other women in this town who
have always been so judgmental of me.

Although Madeleine is only in her mid-thirties, she
seems much older than that. She is a tall, stout woman
who sways from side to side like a big bear. And she
walks with an old hickory cane that belonged to Will's
grandfather. (But I feel she uses this cane more for
effect than physical distress, for she certainly isn't
weak.)

She has coarse, curly blonde hair, which she
obviously dyes, and wears orange/red lipstick that
perfectly matches her long fingernails. She dresses like
some "demimonde" from the 1930s, and her clothes are
quite a sight. But when Madeleine peers at you with
those steel blue eyes of hers, it's as though she sees
your soul. I don't believe I've ever encountered anyone
as strong-willed and intimidating as Madeleine Pou
Bacon, and though Will swears she's the bossiest white
woman he's ever known, there's something special
about her that I can't quite describe.

It's like Madeleine tries to hide a soft soul inside
her for fear someone will think she's weak and take
advantage of her. Will confided to me, before she
joined us at the lunch table, that Madeleine had a tough

childhood and has always had to work, so that's why she's so bossy. But I felt like she was a kindred spirit and saw right through her toughness. Maybe that's why Madeleine and I hit it off so well? And I don't care if Will Bacon married Madeleine for Stanley Pou's money—she takes good care of Will, and that's all that matters to me.

I called Will this morning at the printing shop and asked him and Madeleine to join me for lunch downtown at McGuire's Grill.

"I don't like to eat here," Will said, loud enough for everyone to hear as soon as the three of us walked inside. "The food is always cold and bland. Why did you choose a dump like this, Emily? The people here are so common."

"Really, Will," I said. "Please don't cause a scene in here. There's a table over there against the wall. Let's go sit down before it's taken."

Will and I took a seat at the table while Madeleine spoke to an elderly couple seated in a booth near the front. "God, that woman knows more *old* people—it's the craziest thing I've ever seen!" Will said. "She'll probably invite those two hicks over for dinner Saturday night or something ridiculous like that. I really wish Madeleine would be more *discreet* with whom she chooses to take up."

"Perhaps Madeleine is attracted to people she feels sorry for, Will."

"Don't be so sassy, Emily; it's really not your style." Then, after Madeleine swaggered over to our table, Will quickly stood up and said, "Here's my dear! Please, sit down, my dove. Let me take your walking cane. So, who was that charming couple you were speaking to over there?"

"The Petermans. Stanley and I used to buy some watermelons from their farm when he was still living—and they don't like you either, William, so sit down and order me a beer. I'm dying of thirst."

"Certainly, my dear. And what kind of beer would you like today?" Will asked.

"The usual—and make it two. I don't want tea with my meal."

"Yes, dear. Emily, will you join Madeleine and me for a beer?"

"No, not for lunch. I'll just have iced tea."

"So, Emily Hodge," Madeleine looked at me and said, "I understand you were at that colored political meeting two Saturday nights ago?"

I swallowed the lump in my throat and almost responded with a meek, "Yes, ma'am; I'm afraid so." But then I noticed something in her eyes—a quick look of encouragement. I looked at Madeleine and said, very firmly, "Yes, I was. That's why I wanted to talk to you both today." Then I said, looking at Will, "Our friend, Wilma Watson, who spoke at that meeting—it concerns her."

Will broke in. "Don't be so assuming, Emily. Wilma Watson is *your* friend, not mine. You're the one who chooses to still hang out with that person, not—"

"Be quiet, William," Madeleine said. "I want to hear more about Miss Watson. I understand she one of the 'organizers' of those colored people. She's supposed to teach at that new Negro high school, correct?"

"Yes, and she'll be a good one. Wilma will teach American history and government, in all three grades."

"Educated?" she asked, curiously.

"Very much so, Madeleine. Wilma has a teaching degree from a distinguished teacher's college in Pennsylvania. She also graduated with honors from Tougaloo."

"That Dr. Aaron Geisenberger paid for, no doubt," Will offered, rolling his dark blue eyes in disgust.

"Yes, Will, Mrs. Geisenberger and Aaron *did* pay Wilma's way through both college and teaching school, but Wilma is paying Aaron back—every penny."

"And does that include the green Chevrolet?" he asked, smugly.

"William," Madeleine said, "why don't you just go get us some beers out of the cooler? I don't think that little waitress has noticed us yet." (Though I was sure everyone in McGuire's was *keenly* aware of our presence.) "And make sure my beers are cold!" Then she said to me, "I really need to work on that boy's attitude, don't you agree, Emily?"

"Will means well, Madeleine. Sometimes he just doesn't think before he says things."

"I hate to say this, but I don't know why I married William—I really don't. Guess I've always liked a challenge." Then she added, while she waited for Will to bring the beers back, "And just between us gals, he's *terrible* in bed." After he returned with three bottles of beer, Madeleine took a long deep swallow from hers, set the bottle down loudly on the table, then asked me, "How come a nice white girl like you hangs out with a colored girl like Wilma Watson?"

"I've always wondered that myself, Madeleine," Will commented.

"Be quiet, William, and drink your beer. So—how

come, Emily?"

"Wilma is my best friend, Madeleine, and I don't choose friends by the color of their skin or—"

"I like this girl, William," Madeleine interrupted. "How come you've been hiding her from me?"

"Thank you, Madeleine," I said. "You know, you're very, very—"

"Honest, dear. I'm honest with people. Always have been. Damn near got me killed once, but I always have been." Then she took another gulp of her beer.

The waitress came over and took our order, and I've never seen a female order as much food to eat as Madeleine Bacon did: two cheeseburgers, a large order of onion rings, and some okra and tomatoes that Madeleine made the waitress swear were fresh. "Bad okra gives me the worst gas," she explained. Then she ordered a large piece of pecan pie with ice cream on it for dessert, and she ate it all like a starving dog.

"That was *excellent*," she told both Will and me as she wiped her orange/red lips with a white paper napkin. "Now, let's talk more about Wilma Watson. Is she still in the county jail?"

"No. Sheriff Creel released both her and Reverend Washington last Monday morning."

"I'm not so sure that's good," Madeleine quickly said, exchanging a knowing glance with Will.

"Yeah," Will said. "Wilma should have stayed put in the brig."

"I'll do the explaining, William, if you don't mind."

"I don't understand, Madeleine. Why would it be better if Wilma had stayed in jail? If Wilma were still in jail, she couldn't—"

"Listen to me, Emily Hodge. You need to realize what's happening here," Madeleine said. "There are forces at work in this damn town that I don't think you understand."

Madeleine took the last swallow of beer from her second bottle before she continued, "That new mayor we have—he's in this deep with all the rest of them. I overheard two of our young printers talking down in the basement last week. One of them definitely said Mayor Holmes is a member of the Group."

"The 'Group'? What 'Group'? I don't know what you're talking about, Madeleine."

"He claimed they have regular meetings, every other week, out at Harlan Scruggs' place, south of town. Don't know how many of them there are who meet out there, but I think they meet on Friday nights."

"At midnight!" Will interjected, eagerly. "The witching hour! That's when they all meet out there!"

"I still don't understand what—"

"They're dangerous, child." Madeleine looked at me firmly and said, "Real dangerous. And mean. Every one of them. I grew up with most of those boys. Don't know the ones from town very well. But Homer Holmes—hell, he may be the mayor now and live in that fancy house 'cross from the new theatre, but he's still a farm boy, just like the rest of them.

"Had to fight half those boys when I was growing up. Some of 'em I could lick; some of 'em I couldn't, but I know them all, just the same. And they know about you and Wilma Watson—'specially her. They don't like Negroes who cause trouble—particularly educated ones like Wilma who can stir up all the rest. They're scared of Negroes like that, but they're also evil, Emily. And they're out there waiting—just biding their time—like the devil, himself."

"Are you trying to tell me, Madeleine, that Wilma is in trouble?"

"Emily has always been slow, Madeleine. Sweet, but slow. You just have to keep—"

"Shut up, William. I'm telling you, dear, you *both* are in trouble. They're watching you, Emily. Know for a fact that one of their redneck friends recently moved in across the street from you."

"This group of men you referred to earlier—are they the same ones who murdered Walter Malone?"

Madeleine didn't answer me. She picked up her cane and pointed it at the beer cooler across the room. "William, go get me another beer, please. I see I've got some explaining to do."

That's when I first noticed them—Eddie Scruggs and his cousin, Nolan, had walked inside and were buying some cigarettes from Mr. McGuire's youngest son, who was behind the cash register. I guess I had been listening so intently to Madeleine talk about this mysterious "Group" that I didn't notice them at first, but then Nolan Scruggs saw Will leave the table to go get Madeleine another beer. He tapped Eddie on the shoulder to turn around, and I heard Eddie Scruggs say, "Well, well, Nolan—look who's here." They both just smiled like two hyenas as they watched Will Bacon walk back to our table with another beer and sit down.

I knew Madeleine must have seen them too, but she went right on talking as if she couldn't care less. Then Will saw them walking over to our table, and he got as white as the paper napkin next to his plate.

I instantly picked up on Will's fear. I've never seen

Will Bacon at a loss for words before. Maybe it was because Madeleine was still rambling about old Harlan Scruggs and the Group when Eddie and Nolan stopped at our table, but I could tell Will was terrified of them.

Then Eddie Scruggs said, "I'll be damn, Nolan! Look who all we have sitting here. Sissy little Will Bacon and his fat old wife." Then he looked down at me and said, "And Emily Hodge. How you doin' today? You still hanging around with Wilma Watson and all those other n——s, causing trouble?"

Will looked up at Eddie and Nolan Scruggs and mumbled, "You son of a bitch."

"What'd you say, Navy boy? You say somethin' to me? Sounds like we're gonna have to teach this guy another lesson, Nolan." Nolan nodded his head in agreement.

There was dead silence. Then several of the customers in the Grill got up and began to leave. Out of the corner of my eye, I noticed Mr. McGuire's son nervously calling someone on the phone behind the cash register.

"William," Madeleine calmly said, again patting her mouth with her napkin, "I'm surprised at you. That's no way to address a fellow veteran like Edward Scruggs. Would you hand me my cane, please, William? I need to stand up for a second."

It all happened so quickly that I don't remember who Madeleine hit first with her hickory cane—Eddie or Nolan. Nolan Scruggs fell backward into the metal table behind us, and Eddie dropped to the floor on his knees, both hands clutching his right eye.

"You damn bitch!" Eddie screamed in pain, blood pouring down his face. "You've knocked my eyeball out!"

"And I'm gonna knock the other one out if you two assholes don't get the hell outta here—*now*!"

Will Bacon just sat there like a zombie, his face still white and his mouth wide open.

"I mean it, Eddie!" Madeleine hollered at him again. "Pick that sorry cousin of yours up and hightail it out of here, now!"

"My God, Madeleine!" I shouted. "Are you all right?"

"Sure, I'm fine," she said, examining the end of her walking cane. "But that little bastard Nolan broke it with his hard head. It'll never support *me* again, that's for sure."

"I'll buy you another one, dear," Will finally managed to say. "*Two* of them."

I assumed the McGuire boy must have called Sheriff Creel because I saw his patrol car pull up outside, just as the two Scruggs cousins were staggering out the front door, both of them bleeding profusely. Most of the other patrons inside the Grill had returned to their seats by the time Sheriff Creel and one of his deputies walked inside. He saw the three of us standing next to our table by the wall, and he calmly walked over and removed his sweat-stained hat. He looked at me rather strangely for a few seconds before he said, "I'm sorry."

"Oh, don't be, Sheriff Creel," I replied. "I'm glad you arrived when you did, but I don't think you could have gotten here any sooner or prevented this. We're okay—really. A little shaken up, perhaps, but you should have seen how Mrs. Bacon defended us with her cane! Why, if she hadn't—"

"No, Emily, that's not what I mean," he said. "That's not why I've come. Your mother told me I might find you here. It's about your friend Wilma Watson. She's dead."

He was incomprehensible. He kept on talking, rambling about how they had just found Wilma's car crashed in a ditch off the side of some old dirt road that she shouldn't have been on. But I didn't believe him. Couldn't and wouldn't believe him. Not a word he said! He must be wrong or crazy, or else I had to be in some horrible dream….

"Miss Emily," I finally heard him say. "I need you to go with me to tell her momma. She doesn't know yet."

Having to ride with Sheriff Creel and his deputy to tell Geneva Watson that her precious daughter and my best friend was dead was one of the hardest things I've ever done. I haven't cried like that since I buried our little boy.

My heart is broken forever.
Emily

July 14, 1949

Dear Harry:

Today I buried the best friend I have ever known. Wilma was like a dear sister to me, and when Reverend Washington finally closed the lid on her pine casket and I could see her sweet thin face no longer, something inside me screamed out for revenge. I was utterly and uncontrollably consumed with hatred for the bigotry and ignorance that killed her, and I cursed God in my heart for allowing such injustice in His world!

On the way back from Geneva's house last week, Sheriff Creel explained how someone had probably followed Wilma home from church on Wednesday night. Why she didn't go straight home to Geneva's and was speeding down that dark country road is still a mystery. Sheriff Creel thinks that when Wilma realized she was being followed, she probably tried to lose whoever was tailing her and took a different route than driving north up Leonard Avenue toward the colored part of town where she and Geneva lived.

But why her car was found headed south on Buckner Road toward the Scruggs property at Pine Bluff is unexplainable. Sheriff Creel estimated Wilma's car was traveling seventy-five miles an hour when it missed that curve and left the road. Her Chevrolet struck a huge poplar tree head on, and Wilma was thrown through the windshield. Coroner Taylor said that Wilma probably died instantly, but that's little consolation, knowing how terrified she must have been to be driving that fast at night down an old dirt road.

Wilma was definitely being followed. A colored man who was riding into town that evening recognized her green Chevrolet as it flew past him. He told the sheriff that twenty yards behind Wilma, a new red pickup was flashing its headlights on and off and speeding up "real fast," like it was trying to catch Wilma's car. When the red truck drove past him, the old man said he saw three white men in the cab, but there was no way he could identify them. Not that it would have mattered, because Wilma Watson's death was officially ruled an accident by Coroner Taylor.

Harry, I can't tell you how much it breaks my heart to know Wilma died like that—frightened and all alone. Looking down at her frail body lying in that casket, wearing the white poplin dress that Madeleine and I had bought for her, I couldn't help but feel righteous indignation for the rest of the poor Negroes in that church. Geneva and Wilma's brothers and sisters, cousins, aunts, and uncles were trying so hard to be strong. But then Geneva broke down, ran up to Wilma's coffin, and grabbed her daughter's face in her old hands and began screaming and crying, "My baby! My baby! They done killed my precious baby Wilma!" I cried so hard that I wanted to die.

Some of the men got up and helped Geneva back to her pew. She was totally distraught, and it was a scene I shall remember the rest of my life. When I recall the grief I felt over losing our little boy, who I had known for only a day, it seems so pale now compared to what Geneva is going through. How shallow my loss was next to hers, and I am remorseful for ever feeling sorry for myself.

Madeleine and Will Bacon drove me to Wilma's funeral and sat beside me in the pew. No one spoke during the twenty-minute drive out to the Cemetery Hill Baptist Church, and though Will would never have said so, I could tell he was genuinely grieved over Wilma's death.

The two of us followed Madeleine in as she made her way to the front of the church, took a seat in the first pew on the right, and hung her new walking cane over the back of the long hard bench. (I would have never been so presumptuous as to sit in the front pew of a colored church that I had never been in before, but Madeleine walked right in and sat down like she was a deaconess.)

Madeleine was dressed like she was going to a New Orleans Mardi Gras ball instead of a funeral, and she attracted quite a few stares. Reverend Washington was kind to recognize and thank Mr. and Mrs. Bacon and me for coming out, and he said how grateful Wilma's family and friends were for Christian white folks like us, paying their respects to the bereaved.

Reverend Washington told Geneva and her family that "the Lord works in mysterious ways." Madeleine leaned over and whispered in my ear, "That's for damn sure, honey," when he said that. But then she reached down and squeezed my hand and held it so tenderly in hers that it was hard to believe I had witnessed Madeleine almost kill Eddie and Nolan Scruggs seven days ago. What a curious paradox Madeleine Pou Bacon is to me. How can one human being be so strong and tough, yet so kind and gentle? I admire her so much and pray I were more like her. God willing, one day I shall be!

Then Reverend Washington shouted to the entire congregation, "Wilma Watson—Jesus knows that name!"

"Hallelujah, Brother—Amen!"

"Sister Watson—Jesus knows that name!"

"Hallelujah, Brother—Amen!"

"Teacher Watson—Jesus knows that name!"

"Hallelujah, Brother—Amen!"

"Don't let Wilma Watson's death have been in vain!"

"No sir, Brother—Amen!"

"Don't let Sister Watson's life have been in vain!"

"No sir, preacher!" all the Negroes shouted back. "Hallelujah, Amen!"

"And don't let Teacher Watson's message have been in vain!"

"No, sir, Preacher Washington! Hallelujah—Amen!"

"She spoke out 'bout Walter Malone's murder—that's how come she died!"

"Amen!"

"She spoke out for poor colored folks like us—that's how come she died!"

"Amen!"

"She got up here and say, 'Rise up, my people, and speak out in His name!'—that's how come she died!"

"Amen, preacher. Amen!"

And then I remembered Wilma's "special dream" about walking through a beautiful field of green clover and seeing that big circle—her "rising place," as she called it, where she could stand and raise her palms to

God, and all those bright-colored balloons would start rising up from the ground into the sky—higher and higher. And she was the only one who could stand in that circle and make all those balloons rise up to Heaven.

And it occurred to me what Wilma's dream must have meant: Wilma had encouraged all these poor Negroes to rise up and speak out for the first time in their lives. Watching all of them in that church stand up and shout, "Amen!" while Reverend Ernest Washington spoke to them about freedom and justice, I was proud that Wilma Watson had been my best friend.

Then Reverend Washington said, "Wilma even went to jail on 'count a what she believed!"

"Amen, Brother!"

"And so did Saint Paul, good people—but Saint Paul also say...." Reverend Washington put on his tiny wire glasses and read from an old Bible he pulled from his coat pocket. "This light affliction of ours, which is but a moment, worketh for us a *far* more exceeding and eternal weight of glory."

And all the Negroes in that colored church shouted a loud and resolute, "Amen, brother!"

Driving back home with Will and Madeleine this afternoon in her red Cadillac, I also remembered that sermon I once heard Father Bruni give before the War when I used to attend the Catholic Church here. As I've written you before, he spoke to us about "forgiveness" toward other people who have hurt us greatly.

I believe Wilma would want me to forgive those evil men who caused her death. For her sake I will try, but I can never forget what they did to her.

Emily

5 August 1949
14 Ranier Street
Gary, Indiana

Dearest Emily,

When you stepped off that bus at the Greyhound Station in Gary, and I saw your sweet face again, I realized what a fool I've been all these years. How could I have lost a love like yours? I have no excuse, only regret.

How I had hoped we might still share a new life together, but you were right—we both have changed. You have grown so much and left me behind, and jaded memories are nothing to build a future on. God knows you deserve more than that.

I don't blame you for not wanting to stay in Indiana. People here are so cold and indifferent, and you would be as out of place in Gary as I was in Hamilton. You are a warm, beautiful woman with your whole life ahead of you; I am content to have lived mine. The steel plant where I'm working now fulfills me, but I would gladly exchange it for your love and the chance to try again.

I will always remember these few days that I shared with you. I'm probably crazy for not begging you to stay or going back with you on that bus, but I respect your decision to leave.

I'm truly sorry this didn't work out, Emily—but

it's not your fault; it never was.

Love always,

Harry

P.S. It's best you took your box of letters back with you. I couldn't handle reading them again—knowing I've lost your love forever. H.R.D.

Finally, there was this last letter, which was typed. Other than Harry's January 1942 telegram to Streete and Streete's June 1949 telegram to Emily, it was the only typed letter I found in Miss Emily's old sewing box.

December 21, 1949

Miss Emily Hodge
110 Monmouth Ave.
Hamilton, Mississippi

Dear Miss Hodge:
I am happy that the Commerce Bank of Memphis was able to make a significant contribution to the "Wilma Watson College Fund," which you have started. Your noble efforts will go a long way to ensure that some young man or woman will have a head start in life, armed with a prestigious college degree. Congratulations!
Sincerely yours,
M. Streete Wilder
Vice-President
Commerce Bank of Memphis
P.S. I look forward to being with you again soon, my sweet. Last weekend with you in Memphis was *wonderful*! I can't wait to see you in Hamilton on Christmas Eve. I have lots of presents that I know you will love—one, in particular. And it's just your size!
Love,
Streete

A word about the author...

David Armstrong was born and raised in Natchez, Mississippi. A former mayor and recovering attorney, *The Rising Place*, David's debut novel, was previously made into a film and is currently available on DVD.

He has written two other novels and four screenplays, and when he isn't working his daytime job as COO for the City of Columbus, Mississippi, David is working on his fourth novel.

He is the father of two grown sons, William and Canon, and lives in one of the oldest and most haunted antebellum homes in Columbus.

Thank you for purchasing
this publication of The Wild Rose Press, Inc.

For questions or more information,
contact us at
info@thewildrosepress.com.

The Wild Rose Press, Inc.
www.thewildrosepress.com